AFTERSHOCKS

WHAT READERS ARE SAYING

"Loved it! Really, really enjoyed this and I hope there are many more hot firefighter stories in what looks like a very promising series!"
—Laci Paige, author of the Silken Edge novels, on *Aftershocks*

"Highly flammable and unforgettable. My favorite erotic romance of the year. Cayne's debut erotic romance was impossible to put down."
—MsRomanticReads Romance & Erotica Book Reviews on *Under His Command*

"A romantic BDSM story, Kristine Cayne's erotica debut hits all the right spots and set them on fire."
—Provocative Pages on *Under His Command*

"*Under His Command* is an edgy, sassy, and oh-so-sexy novel! In other words, erotica at its sizzling best. Another 5-star achievement from talented author Kristine Cayne!"
—Laura Taylor, 6-Time Romantic Times Award Winner, 2-Time Maggie Award Winner, & RWA RITA Finalist

"This baby gives new meaning to the word HOT! Insanely creative, toe-curling and to top that, an amazing story as well! If this is Kristine's first erotic romance, imagine what she'll think of next!"
—Jackie Munoz on *Under His Command*

"Stock up on ice cubes because this is definitely one sizzling debut.... As rich as a white chocolate cheesecake, Cayne's entrance into the suspense genre is invigorating, explosive and simply intoxicating...."
—*RT Book Reviews*, 4½ stars, Top Pick! on *Deadly Obsession*

"This is a read that will have you staying up late to not only enjoy Alyssa and Remi's out-of-this-world chemistry, but to see what lengths some will go to in order to preserve what they feel is right."
—Night Owl Reviews, 4.5 Stars, Top Pick! on *Deadly Addiction*

ALSO BY KRISTINE CAYNE

Six-Alarm Sexy Series
Aftershocks (Prequel)
Under His Command (Book One)
Everything Bared (Book Two)
Handle with Care (Book Three)
Lover on Top (Book Four)
Baby, Be Mine (Book Five)
Stripped Down (Book Six – coming soon)

Seattle Fire Series
(Six-Alarm Sexy Spin-off)
In His Arms (Book One – summer 2018)

Men of Boyzville Series
(Six-Alarm Sexy Spin-off)
Going All In (Book One)
Wrangling the Cowboy (Book Two – coming soon)

Deadly Vices Series
Deadly Obsession (Book One)
Deadly Addiction (Book Two)
Deadly Betrayal (Book Three)

Other Works
Origins: The Men of MER in *Shadows in the Mist: A Paranormal Anthology*
Guns 'N' Tulips
Un-Valentine's Day

Writing with Dana Delamar

Total Indulgence Series
Her Two Men in London (Book One)
Her Two Men in Tahiti (Book Two) – summer 2018
Her Two Men in Sonoma (Book Three) – fall 2018

AFTERSHOCKS

SIX-ALARM SEXY
PREQUEL

KRISTINE
CAYNE

ACKNOWLEDGMENTS

I'd like to thank all the wonderful people who encouraged me to write this new erotic romance series that I'd been considering for some time. I've always admired the strength and courage it takes to be a firefighter, but I also wanted to acknowledge the hardships that come with such a dangerous profession. I believe the Six-Alarm Sexy series does just that.

To my wonderful husband for your constant support even when I'm far less than a perfect wife because my fingers are glued to the keyboard and my eyes to the computer screen. And to my fabulously talented boys, for showing me that ability has nothing to do with age.

To Dana Delamar for having such enthusiasm for this project and for keeping me focused on weekly deliverables. I hope someday, we'll be writing one of these together!

To Kyle Moore, Public Information Office for the City of Seattle Fire Department, for your patience in answering my numerous questions. Your answers helped make my firefighters and the rescue scenes realistic and exciting.

To the brave men and women of the SFD's Technical Rescue Team. The world is a safer place because of you. Colin, as promised, your namesake appears in Aftershocks and he will appear in later books in this series as well. Stay safe.

To Jackie, Michelle, and Arianne for being fabulous beta readers. Your insights and suggestions made this a stronger book. I can't thank you enough!

Last but definitely not least, to all my readers for taking a chance on a new author. I hope you'll enjoy this venture into the steamier side of romance. Never fear, my stories will always have an HEA.

CHAPTER 1

Seattle, Washington State, July 2014

Resentment burned in Erica Caldwell's chest as she knelt and wiped a tear off her daughter's cheek. Chloe's big blue eyes rimmed with long black lashes—the mirror image of her father's—pleaded with Erica to make everything better.

"I'm sorry, sweetie. I know you were looking forward to staying with Daddy tonight. But he had to... work."

She almost choked on those last words. Jamie kept letting Chloe down, the same way he'd always let her down. The man couldn't ever do anything as planned or on time. He was always cancelling, postponing, or forgetting. Just like he'd forgotten to sign their divorce papers. Again.

"But Daddy said we'd watch *The Little Mermaid* and eat ice cream sundaes in the living room," Chloe whined.

Pulling her daughter close, Erica smoothed her hand through Chloe's brown curls. "We can watch the movie together." Work was piling up and she'd been counting on the free evening to catch up. But Chloe came first. She always would.

A smile lit Chloe's face and she clapped her small hands. "And can we eat ice cream sundaes in the living room, too?"

Erica couldn't help cringing at the thought, but seeing the hopeful look on her daughter's tear-stained face, she caved. "Just this once."

"I love you, Mommy," Chloe said, flinging herself at her mother.

Erica's heart melted as her daughter's warm pudgy arms circled her neck. There was nothing in the world like a child's hug. "I love you too, sweetie." Straightening, she helped Chloe snap up her pink Hello Kitty raincoat, then slipped the small matching backpack over her shoulders.

After popping open her umbrella, they headed out of the daycare, hand in hand. "We have to run over to the courthouse before we go home. I forgot some important papers on my desk." When Erica stepped off the curb to cross the street, her sneaker landed in a puddle, splashing the hem of her pants. Good thing she'd taken a moment to change out of her heels before racing over to pick Chloe up. Her new Vera Wang pumps would have been ruined.

Back on the sidewalk, Chloe pulled her hand free to hop up the steps and into the courthouse lobby. After waving to Mr. Simmons, the security guard, she placed her backpack on the conveyer belt. Chloe had once told Erica he reminded her of a skinny Santa, and given his round face and ever-shiny bald head, Erica had to admit her daughter had a point.

"Now, don't you be working too late tonight, Miss Caldwell," he teased Chloe as he motioned for her to walk through the metal detector.

Chloe laughed as she skipped through it. "Oh we won't, Mr. Simmons. Mommy said I could have an ice cream sundae for dinner."

Simmons turned an arched brow on Erica. Heat rushed to her cheeks. "That's not what I said," she muttered, hurrying after her daughter and away from Simmons. By tomorrow lunchtime, every employee in the courthouse would think she was the worst mom in the county. The way Simmons could go on, he'd probably have child services coming to interview her about her parenting skills. *And it was all Jamie's fault.*

Ushering Chloe into the elevator, she jabbed the fourth floor button. When the doors didn't close fast enough, she punched it again. Chloe stared at her, a puzzled expression on her pretty face. An expression that looked exactly like the one Jamie frequently gave her. A headache began pounding at her temples. And that was Jamie's fault too. Sure, it was irrational, but she didn't care. Right now, she needed to vent. Fumbling in her purse, she pulled out her cell phone and as soon as the elevator doors opened on her floor, she pressed the call button.

Chloe started skipping down the hall. Since the building was empty except for a few stragglers, Erica didn't bother telling her to stop. "Don't go too far, sweetheart. Stay where I can see you."

As if he'd been waiting, Jamie answered immediately. "Rickie, is everything okay?"

The nickname arced through her like an electric shock. "Stop calling me that! You know I hate it."

"You used to like it."

"Well, now I don't," she shot back.

Hearing his weary sigh, she bit her lip to keep from apologizing. She didn't need to try to please him anymore.

"Did you get to the daycare before it closed?" he asked.

Considering he'd barely given her four minutes' notice that he couldn't pick up their daughter, it was a darn good thing the daycare was just across the street from the courthouse. She'd had to race through the halls and jaywalk across the street and still she'd arrived just as the clock struck six. The daycare charged ten dollars for every minute past closing, and the charge doubled every five minutes. He might have money to burn, but she certainly didn't.

She gritted her teeth and took advantage of the fact that her daughter was out of hearing range. "Chloe's upset."

"I'll make it up to her."

"Don't bother."

"What's that supposed to mean?"

"Jamie, life with you is a roller coaster. She's only four years old and already you're making promises you don't keep. It's too confusing for Chloe." And for her. Half the time she didn't know whether to hate him or love him, so as much as the failure of their marriage rankled her, she'd settled on leaving him.

"I'm sorry, Rickie. I just couldn't make it tonight."

"Uh-huh. And why is that? You traded shifts with Hollywood, and there's no big hockey, football, baseball, or basketball game on tonight." She paused and when he didn't comment, she knew.

The bastard had a date. He hadn't even waited for their divorce to be final before going back to his old ways.

Pain stabbed her chest and she had to lean against the wall to catch her breath. After all this time, he shouldn't have the power to hurt her like this anymore. She wasn't like her mother—she could survive without a man. After her father had died, Erica had been shunted from one relative to another, while her mother floundered, unable to care for herself, much less her young daughter. Orphaned at seventeen, Erica had had to dig herself out of the hole her mother had made of both their lives.

Until Jamie's humanitarian mission to Indonesia, Erica had thought she'd been achieving her goal of self-sufficiency. But the emptiness she'd felt after he'd left, the loss that had filled her, said differently. Just like her mother, Erica had allowed herself to become reliant on a man. But no more. She'd used the time he was gone to make changes, to grow and strengthen herself. And good thing too, given how they'd ended up. Not only had she survived without Jamie since their separation, she'd built a happy and secure life for herself and her daughter.

After all that, hadn't she earned her get-out-of-jail free card?

"Which fire bunny is it? I bet it's Belinda. That witch was always trying to get into your bunker pants even when we were still together," Erica spat into the phone.

She shouldn't care. It really didn't matter who he was dating anymore. But no matter how much she tried to convince herself otherwise, she did care. She did want to know. When he didn't respond, she pushed like a sick masochist desperate for pain. "Well?"

"I'm having dinner with Dani."

Oh God. "You're going on a date with a member of your team?" The earth seemed to shift under her feet. "How long has this been going on?"

"Rickie—"

"Forget it." She cut him off. Some things she was better off not knowing. Their relationship was over, and she really didn't want to hear that he'd been cheating on her. She needed a clean break from him—the sooner the better. "Just sign the damn papers."

Silence filled the line.

Pushing off the wall, she looked around. While she'd been caught up in the conversation with Jamie, she'd let Chloe wander off. Her office lay just around the corner, thirty yards away. Chloe loved the whiteboard. She'd probably raced ahead to draw a nice picture for her. Hurrying down the hall, she covered the mouthpiece and called, "Chloe? Sweetie?"

"I can't sign them," Jamie said, his voice thick with something she couldn't identify.

Was he having second thoughts? When a spark of hope made her traitorous heart flutter, she swore silently. Jamie was bad for her. They were bad for each other. "Why not?"

"I lost them."

"I thought you'd only forgotten to sign them. How could you lose them again?" She'd already had to go through the trouble of getting new certified copies and delivering them to him once. "Enough with the games, Jamie. You don't want me and I don't want you. Find the papers and sign them."

The floor shifted again, rippling before her eyes, and this time, she knew it wasn't just due to her emotional state.

Earthquake.

She had to find Chloe. Now.

Swaying, she staggered around the corner and shouted for her daughter. "Chloe!"

No answer.

"Where are you, Chloe? Answer me! This isn't funny."

All she heard was the groaning of the old building. No one was in the hall, so Chloe had to be in her office. Hopefully, she'd remembered Jamie's earthquake training: drop, cover, and hold on. Erica propelled herself into her office. The room was empty. Her lungs seized and her stomach bottomed out. Where was her daughter?

80 🚋 03

Jamie Caldwell shot to his feet as a wave seemed to warp the floor of the firehouse kitchen. With one hand, he braced the big pot of spaghetti sauce simmering on the stove. His other hand gripped the phone. "Rickie! Erica! What's going on?"

No answer. No sound. Nothing.

He checked the screen. Great. The call had dropped. The tremor ended and he blew in relief, glad it was just a small shake-up. Before enrolling Chloe in the daycare across the street from the courthouse, he'd made sure it was up to the most recent earthquake codes. Erica and Chloe were safe there. He couldn't say as much for the old courthouse where Erica worked. Following the big Nisqually quake, the building had been seismically retrofitted, but two years ago, they'd discovered weak spots in several of the carbon-fiber wraps used to reinforce support columns throughout the courthouse.

While the city and county governments agreed that the retrofitting needed to be redone, in a move typical of Seattle's political squabbling, the project had been put on hold until they could decide which department would pay for the work. He'd told Erica he didn't want her working there, told her it wasn't safe. Lot of good it had done. She'd dug her heels in. In fact, he was pretty sure that was the exact reason she'd accepted the position of administrative specialist with the King County Prosecutor's Family Support Division.

Quickly he dialed Rickie's number. They weren't at the courthouse, but he needed to know they were okay. Her voice had sounded more than a little anxious when she'd called for their daughter.

Instead of a ringtone, he got a fast busy signal. The circuits were no doubt overloaded with people calling to check on their loved ones. People like him. Damn. He'd keep trying until he got through.

He dropped back into his chair and his gaze landed on the papers he'd been staring at for the last hour. The divorce papers. He'd lied to Rickie to stall for time. Once he signed on the dotted line, his marriage would be over forever. And he wasn't sure he wanted that. Wasn't sure at all.

Flipping through the pages, he stopped at the one outlining his visitation rights. In an utterly unsurprising move, Erica was suing for full custody of Chloe. She'd graciously consented to him seeing his daughter for one weekend a month and one day a week according to his work schedule. At that rate, by the time his daughter was in elementary school, she wouldn't even remember she had a father.

Damn the woman.

"Hey, LJ! Did you feel the quake?" He looked up when he heard Dani's excited voice. The team, Battalion 5's Platoon A, had started calling him LJ, short for Lord James, when he'd let slip that he'd been named after his ancestor James Caldwell, the fourth son of Viscount Kensworth.

A sharp bark announced the arrival of Coco, Dani's chocolate Labrador Retriever and the reason for Dani's nickname, K9. The search-and-rescue dog nudged Jamie with her muzzle until he rubbed her ears.

"Did that little tremor scare you?" he asked the dog.

Dani reached into the cupboard and pulled out a box. "Coco's a bit jumpy. Thought I'd give her a treat."

At the word "treat," Coco skidded across the linoleum to get her chew stick. After filling a bowl with water and placing it on the floor, Dani turned to Jamie. "I just read the report. It was a 4.0, epicentered in the south Puget Sound, about six miles deep."

"The Seattle fault's been really active. I hope we're not in for the 'big one.'" He chuckled, making air quotes. "Any damage reports?"

"None so far." She pulled out a chair and sat at the table across from him. "What're those?"

"Divorce papers."

"Ah. I see."

He turned the papers over and leaned back in his chair. "What exactly do you see, K9?"

At the harshness in his tone, she held up her hands and stood. "Nothing at all. Forget I said anything."

Jamie rubbed the back of his neck and looked at his friend. They'd been working together for three years, and he'd put his life in her hands more than once. It wasn't fair for him to transfer his anger to her.

Anger and fear.

Yeah, he had to admit it. He was scared shitless. If the divorce went through, he wouldn't just be losing his wife—he'd be losing his daughter too. "Sorry. You didn't deserve that. I'm just a little tense. Rickie and I were arguing when the quake happened. The call dropped and I haven't been able to get through since."

"You're worried."

"Yeah, it's still no excuse."

"I'm a big girl, LJ. I can take it." She laughed, and he returned her smile. It must have been a damn sucky smile, because she immediately sobered. "You don't want the divorce."

"It's not that clear-cut."

"Why not? You love Erica."

"What makes you say that?"

She tapped his hand. "You've been separated for almost a year, and you're still wearing your wedding ring. I'd say the answer's pretty obvious."

He couldn't help the snort that rumbled up from his chest. "Loving her has never been the problem."

She checked her watch. "Hollywood isn't here yet, so we've got some time. Want to talk about it?"

"I should just sign the damn papers and get it over with." He shrugged and checked on the spaghetti sauce he was cooking for the evening clutch meal. When Hollywood, Platoon C's lieutenant, had agreed to fill in for the second half of Jamie's shift, Jamie hadn't even bothered to ask him to take on his kitchen duties. The man's cooking was so god-awful, Hollywood was likely to give the whole team food poisoning.

"But you don't want to sign them."

"I love Erica and Chloe. But..." He hesitated, unsure he should be spilling the gory innards of his marriage into his friend's lap.

She prompted him. "But...?"

He took out a clean spoon from the utensil drawer and sampled the sauce. After adding a touch more salt, he stirred the simmering mixture and returned to his seat. Seeing the expectant look on Dani's face, he sighed. She wasn't going to let this go. "We don't get along. Two more opposite people don't exist."

"Erica is who she is. Why's it bothering you now?"

"Things have changed in the last few years. She's changed."

"How so?"

"When Chloe was born, she became the center of Erica's world, and I..." He shook his head and trailed off. Even

8

thinking the words made him sound—and feel—like an ass.

"And you were jealous."

"Yes, dammit. But not of Chloe."

"I don't understand."

"At first, I'd take care of Chloe while Erica was resting. I loved giving her a bottle. Bath time was our favorite. I'd bundle her up in a warm towel and rock her until she fell asleep. When she got a little older, I'd read her a bedtime story, whenever I was home." He rose from his chair and got a bottle of water out of the fridge. He held it up and when Dani nodded, he tossed it to her and grabbed another for himself.

"Sounds nice."

"It was." He returned to his seat and opened his bottle, taking a long drink. "Remember when we went to Indonesia on that humanitarian mission?"

"How could I forget? I thought we'd never make it back."

"Yeah, we were gone long enough for Erica to realize she didn't need me. When I got back, she'd taken over and there was no place for me in her life or Chloe's."

Dani's eyes rounded, and she set her bottle on the table. "Christ, Jamie. All this time and you never said a word. Did you at least tell Erica it bothered you?"

"We argued about it, but what could I really say without sounding like a whiny ungrateful bastard? Chloe was happy and healthy, and Erica was taking great care of her."

"But you missed it."

"Hell yeah."

Coco finished her treat and laid her head on Dani's lap. Absently, Dani scratched her ears while frowning at Jamie. "Isn't Chloe staying with you on your days off?"

"That was the original agreement, which only lasted a couple months. In her infinite wisdom, Erica decided it was too disruptive for Chloe to be pulled out of daycare during the week."

"But you could bring her there in the morning and pick her up in the afternoon. You'd still get time with her."

He shook his head. Erica had immediately shot down that idea.

"You're shitting me." Dani stared at him, disbelief clear on her face. "When do you see her?"

"Once a week, on a day Erica decides, I get to pick Chloe up at the daycare at closing time and bring her back the next morning. Once a month, I get a weekend. She stays with me for forty-eight hours."

"Exactly?"

"Not a minute more, not a minute less."

She frowned at him. "When did you become such a doormat?"

"Excuse me?"

"I don't get it. At work, you're the man in charge. But you're letting her push you around. She decides what's what, and you just nod your head."

Put that way, he sounded like a wuss. He shifted in his seat and the creak of the wood sounded ridiculously loud. "It's not like that. I thought it would make her happy if I went along with things."

"Congratulations. Now you're both miserable. Even I, the queen of failed relationships, can see that you need to man up and tell her what you want. Otherwise, accept that your marriage is over, sign the papers, and move on."

"I know."

"But you haven't made up your mind yet."

He grinned. "I told her I lost the papers. Twice."

"Now that's not too hard to believe." She tossed her bottle cap at him. "You need to stop playing games, LJ. Seriously, get your head out of your ass before you lose your family."

That was why he'd cancelled on Rickie. He had some serious decision-making to do and until he made up his mind, he couldn't see her. It would just confuse him more. They'd end up arguing and he'd be caught in a sort of turned-on frustrated state. He needed some alone time to decide what he was going to do—sign or don't sign—and the Caldwell family cabin, secluded as it was in the Cascade Mountains, was just the spot to do some serious thinking.

He probably shouldn't have lied to her about his plans, shouldn't have implied that his dinner with Dani was a date. But he hadn't been able to resist one last attempt to spark some jealousy in her. He'd sparked something all right—anger. He just wished he'd been there. Erica was exceptionally beautiful when her brown eyes burned with indignation. He smiled, recalling some of their more memorable fights and the make-up sex that had followed.

From that first night, she'd grabbed him by the balls, turning his world upside down. Hollywood, his best friend, had dragged him to a party a friend of his cousin's was giving. The party was big and wild. He'd been about to leave when he spotted the beautiful blonde across the room. After confirming that she wasn't a fire bunny, he approached her with every intention of trying to charm her into a great one-night stand.

And boy did he succeed. She was fun and fascinating, and even before the night was over, he knew he wanted more.

But the next morning, he'd woken up to find her side of the bed cold and empty. They hadn't exchanged phone numbers or last names, so he'd had no way of contacting Rickie. Determined to see her again, he'd bullied Hollywood into trying to track her down through his cousin, but that had gone nowhere. In the end, he'd nursed his crushed heart with a ballgame and a six-pack.

When she'd knocked on his door a month later to tell him he was going to be a father, he'd been stunned by the news, but happy that whether she wanted it or not, Rickie was going to be in his life.

Dani rapped her knuckles on the table and Coco barked, drawing him out of his reverie. "It's been my experience that these things aren't usually one-sided. My dad was pretty hands-off when I was little, and I see my cousin Joe doing the same thing with his own kids. His wife does everything, and believe me, she isn't at all happy about it."

His shoulders stiffened. "Are you saying I intentionally let Rickie take over?" Ridiculous.

"Didn't you?"

A film of sweat formed on his brow. "No. Of course not."

"You never went home late so you wouldn't have to deal with the morning routine? You never told Erica you were out on a call just so you could go to a sports bar after work to have breakfast and catch a ball game with the guys? Come on, Jamie. I know you did."

Coco's sudden growl put them both on guard. "What's wrong,

girl?" Dani asked as she tried to calm the dog. But Coco wasn't having it, and her growls turned to barks and whimpers.

Jamie gulped down the rest of his water, glad for the distraction. He should have known better than to talk about this with Dani. The woman loved to psychoanalyze the guys on the team and push their buttons. Sometimes she did it just for fun, though this time, she seemed to really believe what she was saying. But she was wrong. He wouldn't have let Rickie push him out of Chloe's life, even subconsciously. What kind of man would let that happen?

Before he could answer his own question, a violent quake shook the stationhouse. Cupboards banged open, dishes crashed to the ground, and the pot of spaghetti flew off the stove. The tangy scent of tomatoes filled the air as the hot sauce splashed across the floor, splattering the fridge, the walls, and the dog. Coco yelped and scampered out of the way.

Dani blanched. "This is no aftershock," she said, as the tremor went on and on.

The firehouse had recently been retrofitted to the highest standards and would survive all but a massive earthquake. That didn't mean they couldn't be hit by flying objects though. In the distance, Jamie heard his team members shouting and prayed no one was hurt.

He scrambled around the table, almost falling when the floor seemed to buckle. Grabbing Dani's hand, he pulled her under the sturdy table with him. Coco slid in between them and Dani wrapped her arms around the dog. They'd be safe here.

But where were Rickie and Chloe? He yanked his cell phone out of his shirt pocket and speed-dialed Erica's number again. When he got another fast busy, he swore and hung up. With a quake this intense, there was going to be some serious damage, and his unit, the Seattle Fire Department's Technical Rescue Team, would certainly be called on to help extricate survivors from collapsed buildings. It could be hours before he had time to call again. At least by now, Rickie and Chloe would be home in the house he'd had built for them. A house that could and would withstand anything.

Or so he prayed.

CHAPTER 2

Adrenaline surging through her system, Erica hung onto the doorjamb as the quake rocked the old courthouse. The building swayed and groaned, windows rattled and shattered as the earth continued to tremble. Cracks raced across the ceiling and plaster dust showered down, covering everything in a thin white film. She'd lived in Seattle all her life but had never experienced a quake as powerful as this one.

And her daughter was all alone.

Erica thrust herself through the open door to her office and back into the hall. Her arms outstretched on either side, she bounced from one wall to the other like a Ping-Pong ball. But at least she was moving in the right direction. Crashes and bangs drew her down the corridor to where most of the offices were located, as well as the large lunchroom. Dear God. Had Chloe gone to check out the offerings in the vending machines?

When she reached the older part of the building and saw the full extent of the damage, Erica's heart shuddered like the courthouse itself. This entire section of the floor looked like a war zone. "Chloe!" she called, her chest contracting so tightly her voice came out a mere squeak. She filled her lungs with the dust-choked air and tried again. "Chloe, where are you?"

Tears burned her eyes and a sob constricted her throat. Chloe was by herself. Alone. Her little girl needed her. And she needed her little girl. Needed to know she was safe.

The shaking finally stopped.

"Thank God." Blinking to clear her vision, Erica picked her way around fallen walls, ceiling tiles, and light fixtures, avoiding bits of sharp metal and live wires that sizzled like rattlesnakes. "Chloe! Can you hear me? Don't move. Don't touch anything. Mommy's coming." She could only pray that Chloe was somewhere safe and not trapped under all the rubble. Or worse.

Where should she start looking? What should she do?

Jamie. Jamie would know. Patting the pockets of her pants, she blew out in relief when her fingers closed around the familiar rectangular shape. Thank goodness she hadn't lost it in the quake. Yanking it out, she quickly dialed Jamie's cell number and waited for the call to connect. Instead she got a fast busy signal. Her fingers trembled as she hung up and tried 911. Still no luck.

Tucking the phone back into her pocket, she straightened her shoulders. Okay. She was going to have to do this on her own, like she did everything. Over the continued groaning of the building and the shrieks of security and car alarms coming in through the broken windows, she called out. "Chloe! If you can hear me, shout. Help me find you." She paused and listened, straining to identify each sound. When there was no reply, she moved further into the wreckage and called again. Bending down, she looked for places Jamie had told her were called voids, those empty areas that already existed or were created by falling debris where a person could be sheltered.

Ahead, an office wall had fallen against another, creating a tunnel. Maybe Chloe was there. Crouching, Erica inched forward, calling out, listening for any sign of movement. A loud crack overhead startled her and she scooted back, falling on her butt. The wall crashed down, missing her by half a foot. Heart pounding, Erica froze. Had she not moved in time, she'd have been crushed. What if something had fallen on Chloe? Oh God. What if her daughter was dead?

Heavy footsteps and shouting from the direction of her office reached her. Pushing to her feet, she called back. "Over here!"

Moments later, Mr. Simmons' bald head appeared around

the corner. His hand went to his chest. "Mrs. Caldwell, thank God. When I got to your office and couldn't find you, I almost had a heart attack." He scanned the area. "Where's your daughter?"

Erica raised her hands, a lump in her throat strangling her. "Somewhere," she croaked. "She raced ahead of me.... We were apart when the quake hit."

He swallowed visibly, his eyes fixed on the rubble that had been the common area. "We'll call in help. But you need to come with me. We're evacuating the building."

Was the man crazy? "I can't leave my daughter!"

"We'll call the firemen. They'll find her."

Not regular firemen, but maybe Jamie. She hadn't been able to reach him by phone but surely the courthouse security had some sort of direct line? "Call my husband. He's with the technical rescue team."

"Okay, but—"

"Shh." She cut him off with an upraised hand. A sound. She heard it again. "Mommy!"

Chloe. She was alive. Before her mind even had time to assimilate the word, her feet were on the move. She climbed over the debris, tearing her pants and scratching her legs and hands, desperate to reach her daughter. "I'm coming, Chloe. Mommy's coming."

Simmons grabbed her around the waist, pulling her to a halt. "Mrs. Caldwell, stop. It isn't safe. The building is unstable."

"Let go of me!" She twisted out of his hold and threw herself out of his reach. Her foot crashed through a downed wall, tripping her. Her arms pinwheeling wildly, she scrambled to right herself. Backing away from Simmons, she moved toward where she'd heard Chloe. "I'm not leaving my child."

The floor vibrated and chunks of plaster fell from the ceiling. When a piece bounced off her head, she stumbled and rammed into a wall. *Damn! Would this earthquake never end?* She had to find her daughter and get them both out of the courthouse before it crumbled to the ground.

"Mrs. Caldwell, please."

Something snapped and a large crack snaked across the ceiling. Dust filled the room as more drywall and several light fixtures shook loose. A boom rent the air and the building trembled. With Chloe's screams echoing in her head, Erica looked up and saw the crack widening. *The ceiling was caving in.* Her mouth went dry and her heart pounded in her ears. Was this the end? Was she never going to see her daughter again? Jamie? She'd made so many mistakes, had so many regrets.

Something—the wall?—landed on her back, knocking her facedown onto the crushed remnants of someone's desk. Instinctively she wrapped her arms around her head and prayed for the chance to make things right for her family.

ഇ 🚒 ൙

The firehouse bells blared in his ears as Jamie crawled out from under the table and offered his hand to Dani. The usually spotless kitchen was a mess, but cleanup would have to wait. An announcement came over the speakers: "Structural collapse rescue, Ladder 27, Rescue 21, and Aid Unit 44 needed at 3rd and James. Multiple victims."

He scooped up the box of Coco's treats he'd almost crushed with his boot and set it on the table. "Better bring these. Looks like it's going to be a long night."

Dani nodded, her face pale, as she tried to soothe the trembling dog. Rising, she took Coco by the collar with one hand and the box with the other. "Let's go."

Racing through the lounge, they grabbed their radios from the battery charging station and made their way to the south apparatus room. Jamie pulled up short when he spotted Hollywood lounging against Ladder 27 in his turnout gear. Jamie could almost see the adrenaline coursing through the man's veins. "Glad you made it. We could use an extra pair of hands."

"I guess you're still in charge?"

He clapped Hollywood on the back. "Yep. I'm bumping you down to driver, Lieutenant." He turned to address the other team members. "Gabe, you're driving Rescue 21."

Once everyone had their turnout gear on, they jumped into their vehicles. Jamie sat in the passenger seat of Ladder 27 while Hollywood got behind the wheel. Dani and Coco took their places in the back compartment. As Hollywood turned on the siren and pulled onto 4th Avenue heading northwest, Jamie twisted around and looked at his younger brother, Drew, behind them in Rescue 21. *Christ*, he wished the kid weren't here. It would be so much easier to focus if he knew Drew were safe at home. As if reading his thoughts, Drew waved, face grim. Since he was in Battalion 5's Platoon B, they didn't usually work the same shifts. Wasn't it a kick in the ass that they were during the worst disaster to hit Seattle since the Nisqually earthquake? Fate was a bitch.

Jamie forced himself to focus. Drew was a member of the technical rescue team because he was qualified to be, more than qualified actually. He would be okay. Facing forward, Jamie got his first look at the chaos that had overtaken his city. Cars parked along the streets were buried beneath piles of bricks and chunks of cement. Broken glass covered the sidewalks, which hadn't fared much better.

Ahead, an oil tanker lay on its side, blocking the width of the road. Worse, smoke rose from the engine and flames licked around the edges of the hood. Hollywood slammed the brakes. "Shit! If that thing blows, it'll take down the neighborhood."

The driver had climbed out and stood in the entrance to a restaurant, watching his truck burn. "We get stuck in that mess, we won't be helping anyone tonight," Jamie said, punching the talk button on the Motorola digital radio attached to his turnout coat, and reported the incident.

"Engine 10 is already en route. ETA two minutes," the dispatcher answered.

"Can you get us around it?" Jamie asked Hollywood as he watched the flames reaching higher. From what he could see, there wasn't enough open space between the parked cars and the tanker for them to pass.

His expression tight, Hollywood nodded. "Shut the windows."

Metal screeched against metal as Ladder 27 pushed through the narrow opening, sending a shudder through Jamie's body. Hollywood cursed as the driver's side mirror caught on the downed truck's bumper and ripped off. Jamie twisted in his seat to watch the progression of his team. The acrid scent of burning paint filled the cabin as the flames grew.

Finally, they made it past the tanker. Rescue 21 and Aid 44

easily drove through the space Hollywood had made for them. When he once again looked down the road, Engine 10 was weaving through the traffic toward them.

Jamie relaxed. His team could concentrate on getting to their destination. And if anyone could get them there in record time, it was Hollywood. Besides being a valuable member of the technical rescue team, the guy had been the best driver in the SFD before becoming lieutenant of Battalion 5's Platoon D.

As he checked the Computer Aided Dispatch View reports on the MDC, the Mobile Data Computer, Jamie's heart almost stopped. How could he not have realized sooner?

Hollywood shot him a look through narrowed eyes. "What's wrong?"

"We're going to 3rd and James," he said, sounding like he'd inhaled a mouthful of dirt.

"That's the King County Courthouse...." Hollywood's voice trailed off as he glanced at Jamie. "Oh fuck."

Oh fuck was right. Rickie couldn't possibly still be at work, could she? No. She and Chloe were at home. Probably scared shitless, but safe. Having left his bunker jacket undone, he fished his cell phone from his shirt pocket and speed-dialed the house. Four rings later, the answering machine picked up. Swearing profusely, he left a message and hung up. Immediately he dialed Rickie's cell phone. No fast busy this time. The phone rang and he held his breath. *Come on, Rickie. Pick up.*

The ringing stopped, but he didn't hear anyone answer.

"Rickie!" he shouted into the phone. When he heard no response, he checked his phone's display. Dammit. The call had died. He tried again and got a fast busy. What the hell did that mean? Had Rickie answered or had it been something weird with the network? She had to be okay. *They* had to be okay. Rickie and Chloe were his whole world.

His radio beeped, startling him. He pressed the talk button. "Caldwell."

"Everything okay, Jamie?" Drew asked, his voice gruff.

His throat tightened at the concern in his brother's tone. Maybe it wasn't so bad that they were on the same team tonight after all. He cleared his throat. "I don't know, kid. I can't reach Rickie."

"It's pretty late. She's probably at home. Did you try there?"

"Yeah. Voicemail."

There was a brief silence and then, mercy of mercies, Drew signed off. Cold fear had already taken root in Jamie's gut, and he didn't need any more of his brother's well-intentioned questions to help it along.

At the corner of 4th and Holgate, the truck came to a complete standstill. Jamie's gaze flew to Hollywood. The intersection was a massive knot, as cars from all directions tried to drive around the multi-vehicle pileup at its center. It would take hours to clear everyone out of the intersection. Wasn't his problem, but getting around it was. "We don't have time for this."

"I know, man," Hollywood said. His expression one of intense concentration, he took a sharp left onto Holgate, swerving around the maze of stopped cars. He rode the truck up onto the sidewalk and blew the horn repeatedly.

Gripping the dash, Jamie closed his eyes and prayed. Prayed for Rickie and Chloe. And prayed that his team made it to the courthouse in one piece.

The crackle of static from his radio filled the cabin before he heard the dispatcher's voice. "Ladder 27."

He pressed the talk button. "Caldwell here."

"A security guard from the courthouse is on the line. I'm patching him through."

A hole burning in his gut, Jamie grabbed the two-way and held it up to his ear. "Roger."

"Hello?" A man's shaky voice came over the radio. "This is John Simmons, head of security at the King County Courthouse. We've got a situation here. How long before you guys arrive?"

Jamie tried to reassure the man. "We're only a few blocks away. Tell me what you've got."

He heard Simmons blow out a breath. "Those damn faulty support columns are buckling. The ceiling on the fourth floor has already caved."

Rickie's floor. His hand crushing the two-way, Jamie wheezed out, "Have you evacuated?"

"Everyone's out except for the security staff and five others."

"Tell me about the five."

"Mr. Perez is trapped in the elevator on the seventh floor

19

outside Interpreter Services. The door to Judge Tennison's office on the third floor west is stuck. Also on the third floor, Mrs. Anders is caught behind some live wires. We're trying to cut the power so we can get her out."

When the man stopped talking, Jamie prodded him. "What about the other two?"

"Woman and child. When the ceiling collapsed, the woman was buried."

His stomach clenched as his unease grew. *No. It couldn't be.* "And the child?"

"She called for her mother before the collapse. Since then, nothing."

He didn't want to hear it, but he had to know. Clearing his throat, he forced a calm, professional tone into his voice. Even though he was dying inside. "What's the woman's name?"

"Caldwell. Said her husband was on the Technical Rescue Team. Said to call him. Can you contact him?"

The words hit him like a sucker punch to the gut. White stars filled his vision and he had to take several deep breaths to regain his equilibrium. "You just did, man," he choked out.

"Mr. Caldwell? Shit, I'm so sorry."

"What floor is my wife on? What's on her? Is she conscious?" And, oh Christ, where was his daughter? Was Chloe even still alive?

"Fourth floor, center. Down the hall from her office."

Dani's small hand squeezed his shoulder. "We'll find them, Jamie," she said gently.

"Damn straight." His gaze slid to Hollywood. "Can you get us there PDQ? Or do I have to get out and hotfoot it?"

"Hang tight!" Hollywood shouted as he pulled a sharp right on to South King Street, gunning past CenturyLink Field. "At least the Sounders aren't playing tonight," he muttered.

The situation would have been pretty near catastrophic with an additional sixty thousand people milling about.

His mind shredded, Jamie stared numbly at the narrow traffic-snarled roads of downtown Seattle. He and his crew were Rickie and Chloe's best chance of surviving this nightmare. They just had to get there before the entire building collapsed, or it was game over.

CHAPTER 3

When Ladder 27 was still a half-block from the courthouse, going north on a south-running one-way, Jamie leaned over and slammed his palm firmly against the horn as Hollywood attempted to weave through the clogged street. People scattered and more than one bird was flipped his way. Tough shit. They were *alive*, whereas his little girl—

Nope. Not going there. Think positive, that's what he had to do. His platoon was the best, and he had to believe that they'd get Rickie and Chloe out safely. Anything else was self-defeating.

But despite Hollywood's best efforts, they were barely moving. Adrenaline spiked in his system and Jamie felt as though he were going to burst out of his skin. Instead, he shoved open the door and jumped out of the truck. Multiple what-the-fuck shouts from his team rang out. Yeah, it was stupid. With all the weight and awkwardness of the turnout gear, he could have twisted an ankle, but shit. His skin was crawling with the need for action, the need to do *something*, no matter how boneheaded.

Sucking in a breath to get himself under control before facing perhaps the worst situation of his life, he beat feet up the road, past City Hall Park to the 3rd Avenue entrance to the courthouse. As Jamie pushed through the rotating door, panting and sweating, a middle-aged bald man who seemed vaguely familiar came up to him. His uniform indicated he was one of the security guards.

"Simmons?" Jamie asked.

The man nodded. "You Caldwell?"

Jamie inclined his head. "Any change since we spoke?"

Simmons motioned to the lobby's darkened overhead lights. "We managed to cut the power and get Mrs. Anders out of the building."

At least that was something. "Anything else I should know about? Leaks? Water? Gas?"

"None that we're aware of."

Not too reassuring given how long it had taken them to find the power main. He swallowed before voicing his next question. "My wife? My daughter?"

Simmons' eyes fell to the floor and a great pressure around Jamie's chest forced him to push his shoulders back to inhale. Damn. He hadn't expected anything different, but he had hoped. "You got guys to take my team to the vics?" His stomach revolted at the word he'd never thought he'd use to refer to his wife and daughter.

Nodding, the old guard said, "Ten plus me."

The ladder truck and Rescue 21 pulled up to the curb with Aid 44 right behind them. As the team assembled, Jamie began giving orders. "Drew, you and Gabe, take the disabled elevator on the seventh floor. Hollywood, take the care of the vic on the second floor. Evan and Colin, grab some of the security team and make sure all the floors are clear. Dani, you and Coco are with me on the fourth floor."

"Hold up a minute." Hollywood stepped close to Jamie and said in a low voice, "You sure you should be leading this?"

Suppressing the urge to ignore his best friend, he shifted his weight back on his heels to keep his feet still. Hollywood wasn't saying anything the captain wouldn't have said if he weren't tied up with the chaotic aftermath of the quake. "I can handle this."

"You know the protocol. You're too close."

Jamie crossed his arms and glared at his soon to be ex-friend. "Fuck protocol."

Hollywood held up his hands. "Fine. But if you change your mind…"

"I won't."

Jamie turned and gave the signal to his team. They secured SCBAs on their backs and hooked faceplates on their heads, but didn't close them. Then they grabbed ropes, pulleys, saws, and anything else they might need based on Simmons' description of the various situations. With Jamie in the lead, they all tromped through the lobby, their boots slapping the floor tiles, and met up with the security team.

"This way, sir," Simmons said, leading the way to the central stairwell. To stay in shape, Jamie and the team often trained in full gear, so going up four flights would be no problem for him and Dani.

But in the dim glow of the emergency lighting, Simmons' flushed face, slick with sweat, told a different story. Shit. Now was so not the time for the old man to rupture an artery or pop a valve. "Everything okay, Simmons?" he asked. "We can go the rest of the way on our own."

Simmons shook his head, and turning the corner, began plodding up the final set of stairs. "It'll be faster if I show you where Mrs. Caldwell is."

With Coco along, Jamie didn't need anyone's help to find his wife, but he understood and even respected the old guy's need to be useful. To a point.

Stepping out of the stairwell onto the fourth floor, Jamie quickly oriented himself. They'd come out on the opposite side from where the elevators were located, closer to the central part of the building than to Rickie's office on the eastern side.

"Were the offices damaged?" he asked the guard.

"Some, but nothing like this area."

Jamie had thought as much. Why hadn't Rickie and Chloe been in her office? "How much farther?"

"It's a little hard to see, but I believe she was"—Simmons moved a few yards ahead and crouched, looking under a plank—"here...." He let the sentence hang, and a bewildered look came over his face.

Worry punched Jamie in the gut. But the old man's confusion wasn't unusual when everything was reduced to a pile of rubble, all visual reference points gone. It did mean they had to spend precious minutes locating Rickie.

Jamie shouted her name, then waited for a response before

calling Chloe's. Nothing. Dani removed Coco's leash and let her loose. As the dog maneuvered almost daintily around the dangerous debris, she sniffed and yipped. And Jamie's speeding heart shifted down a gear. He'd seen Dani and Coco in action many times. Their track record was impeccable.

When Coco's barks intensified, Dani shouted, "She's on to something."

Jamie rushed to them, careful not to fall or, worse, impale himself on the minefield of broken metal, wood, and glass. He knelt next to Coco while Dani ruffled the dog's fur and murmured, "Good girl."

Instead of seeing Rickie or Chloe, he saw a filing cabinet and a fallen wall behind it. Coco wasn't a cadaver dog, so if she'd stopped here, it was because she smelled someone. Someone *alive*.

"Rickie, Chloe!" he called.

When there was no response, he forced himself to put his training into practice and quickly assessed whether the cabinet was supporting the fallen wall. If so, moving it would bring the whole mess down on his wife or daughter—whoever was trapped underneath. After confirming that it was safe to move the cabinet, he lifted it away from the wall very carefully so as not to further destabilize the mound of rubble.

Dani shined her flashlight into the darkness of the void. As Rickie turned her beautiful face toward him, blinking at the light, his heart slammed against his chest like a crazed fly against a bright bulb. Her skin was pale and she had contusions on her face and arms. The rest he'd have to examine once they got her out. The important thing was that they'd found her—alive, but quite clearly trapped.

Lying on her stomach with the wall on her back, she inched a hand out to him. "Jamie," she whispered. "I knew you'd come." A tear slid down her cheek.

Love for Rickie welled in his heart until he thought he'd drown in it. He gripped her fingers and squeezed gently. "Always," he said, his voice gruff.

"Chloe?"

Christ. The hope in her voice pierced his heart. He ran his thumb along her wrist. "We'll find her. Stay still while I get you out of here." With that, he turned to Dani and nodded. She rose and set off with Coco to continue the search.

He laid his equipment and SCBA on the ground before searching the debris for materials to build a crib under the wall. All he needed was to clear a few inches so he could pull Rickie out. He'd lift the wall, angling it along the length of her body.

After finding a heavy chunk of cement to use as a fulcrum, a section of two-inch wide metal pipe, and several pieces of wood he could use for cribbing, he returned to Rickie. Kneeling beside her, he explained what he was going to do. Normally, leveraging and cribbing was done with several people, but he couldn't bring himself to call Dani back. As it was, it was killing him not to be searching for Chloe with her.

Standing at Rickie's head, he cleared out the loose debris and positioned the fulcrum, centering it on the wall. He placed the wood blocks on either side, ready to be pushed into place. The structure wouldn't be as stable as if he put the blocks on the edges of the wall, but this was the best he could do on his own. "I'm going to lift the wall and put the first layer of cribbing in place. Don't move."

He pushed down on the metal pole and, as the wall began to rise, he kicked one of the blocks into place, then the other. Slowly he released the lever until the wall rested on the blocks. A few more layers and he could pull her out. "It's going great, Rickie. We're almost there."

The second layer of blocks went into place easily. The third and final layer would be more difficult to do alone. He wiped the sweat from his forehead with the back of his hand, then bent to position the final set of blocks. Coco's loud bark pierced the relative silence. The hairs on his arms rose at the fear evident in her ensuing growls. He grabbed his flashlight and whipped it around in time to see Coco dashing away from the common area. He pressed the button on his two-way. "Dani, what's wrong with Coco?"

"Last time she did this, the quake hit. Take cover, LJ!"

Fuck! He threw himself on the ground so he could see Rickie. "Cover your head, honey. Something's happening."

Eyes unbelievably round and white in her dirty face, she asked, "An aftershock?"

"Maybe."

The floor began to shake. She swallowed and sucked in a sob. "I'm really scared, Jamie."

The crack in her voice made his heart break. It went against everything he'd ever been taught, but he inched himself forward until he was half under the wall. He rested his head next to hers and held her hands. "We'll get through this." And if they didn't, at least they'd die in each other's arms.

When the aftershock ended, Jamie stayed where he was but very carefully pressed the button on his two-way. "Team, report."

Dani came on first. "Looks like Coco's a good quake alert, LJ. I rewarded her with a treat, and now we're going back to the search."

Hollywood's deep chuckle filled the line. "Next time give us a little more warning, will ya? We're okay here too, LJ."

They waited and the line remained quiet. Fuck. Where was Drew? Working with elevators was always dangerous. Add in an earthquake and it was a recipe for disaster. "Drew? Drew? Come in," he said into the two-way, forcing his voice to remain calm, professional. The last thing he wanted was for the captain or Hollywood to pull him off the mission because his family was involved. Shit. That's exactly *why* he needed to stay.

After endless seconds, he heard the familiar cocky tone of Drew's voice. "Had a bit of a ride when the elevator dropped two floors, but we're okay now."

Blood rushed in his ears as Jamie's chest seemed to collapse in on itself. *Christ. A runaway elevator.* He dropped his forehead against the ground so Rickie couldn't read his reaction. So many people he loved were in this building, their lives and welfare his responsibility. Maybe Hollywood had a point after all.

"Rickie and I are okay, too," he said, once he'd gotten his racing pulse under control.

"Chloe?" Drew asked.

Dani answered. "Nothing yet."

Silence filled the air as everyone absorbed that statement.

Jamie clicked off his two-way and turned his head in the tight enclosure to kiss Rickie's tear-drenched cheeks. "Don't give up," he said firmly.

Her lips trembling, she nodded.

Carefully, he slid himself out from under the wall. The sooner he finished with Rickie, the sooner he could go find his baby girl.

৪০ 🚂 ৫৪

Feeling punch-drunk, Erica lifted her head as much as she could to watch Jamie at work. He'd jerry-rigged some sort of contraption he called a crib to lift the wall. Seeing him looking so competent calmed her, gave her a sense of security. How he managed to push up the wall with the metal pipe and position the blocks under it at the same time she had no idea. His sheer strength amazed her. Maybe they would get out of this after all.

"Almost done, Rickie. I'll have you out in a couple more minutes."

Thank God. She hated that Jamie was stuck getting her free when they should both be looking for Chloe. But maybe she could help move things along.

She kept watch and when he pushed down on the lever to lift up the wall, she rose on her elbows and tried to wiggle her way out.

"No!" Jamie shouted. "Don't move!"

Why not? She was doing it. She was getting herself out. Pushing to her knees, she hit the wall with her back and lost her balance. She thrust her body forward and her arms clipped one of the cribbing blocks Jamie had set up. Oh, jeez.

The blocks on one side—the side she'd hit—tumbled. She screamed as the wall crashed down onto her arm. Through her tears, she saw that Jamie had somehow managed to jam the tumbled blocks under the wall. His quick action had probably kept her arm from being severed. She tried to speak, tried to tell him she was sorry, but no words would form. If he didn't hate her before, he'd hate her now.

"Rickie, are you okay? Talk to me," he said.

"My..." She cleared her throat and tried again. "My arm..." She couldn't speak as a sob of frustration shook her body.

"Your arm is pinned," he finished for her. "Why the *fuck* did you move?"

"I—I wanted to help."

"Are you sure that's it?"

With her free hand, she brushed strands of hair out of her eyes. She got that he was upset, but still. "Of course I'm sure."

"You know what I think," he said as he picked up a block of cement and moved to the side of the wall parallel to her body. She couldn't see him now. But she could hear him just fine. "I think you need to trust me for once in your life. I've been rescuing people for twelve years. I know what I'm doing here."

"I do trust you, Jamie."

"No you don't. Not with this and not with Chloe." He grunted and the wall lifted off her arm. "Can you move your arm? Pull it in next to your body. Slowly."

She followed his instructions. The fit was tight, but she managed to wiggle her arm free. It throbbed but she could move her wrist and fingers. "I got it."

"Good. Stay clear. I'm lowering the wall."

Except for a few inches of dim light ahead of her, she was back to where she'd been when Jamie had found her—trapped in near darkness. "What are you going to do now?"

"We're at square one again. Sit tight." Frustration deepened his voice. Come to think of it, she'd heard that tone more and more over the years. When she'd first met him, Jamie had been so light and carefree. He'd always had a joke to make her smile. She'd been so infatuated with him. Couldn't believe that such a hunk found her attractive. But after Chloe, things had changed. Only he hadn't. Except now, she couldn't remember why his sunny disposition had bothered her so much. She loved his smile. And she missed it.

Jamie cleared his throat. "What were you and Chloe doing here anyway? I was sure you were at home by the time the real quake hit."

She dropped her head onto her uninjured arm and gritted her teeth. Now she remembered. He was amazingly self-centered. "Jamie, you gave me four minutes' notice. Do you honestly think I had time to pack up all my things before picking Chloe up from the daycare? I barely made it before closing as it was."

"Sorry."

"You're sorry we got caught in the quake, but you're not sorry you copped out at the last minute. I'm the one who had to dry our daughter's tears when she learned you weren't coming. We're an inconvenience to you, Jamie. Admit it. Once and for all, just admit that you"—her voice cracked but she pushed the words out—"never wanted us."

"God, babe. That's so not true. I wanted you and Chloe from day one."

She laughed, the sound bitter. "If I hadn't shown up pregnant, we would never have been together. You'd have been perfectly happy with it being a one-night stand. Too bad I wasn't one of your fire bunnies."

"Rickie, I was twenty-eight when we met. I was ready to settle down and have a family. The last thing I wanted was another bunny."

"And see how well that turned out."

"Cover your head," he said before the wall lifted a couple inches.

Jamie slipped another block into place and with each inch closer to freedom, the pressure in her chest eased. "You might not be the best husband, but you're darn good at rescuing people. Thank you."

He cursed and she heard him suck in a deep breath. From his reaction, you'd think she'd insulted him.

"Look, when this is all over, let's go to Disneyland. Chloe will love that."

What the heck? "What are you talking about?"

"We just need a chance to reconnect. To be a family again."

"This is exactly the problem with our relationship, Jamie. You're Peter Pan. Will you ever grow up? We're in the middle of a divorce, and our daughter could be *dead*. I don't want to hear about Disneyland!"

As was usual for him, he didn't say a word. Whenever they argued, he clammed up. Did they mean so little to him that he couldn't even be bothered to fight? The wall rose again and Jamie pushed another block under it on each side of the lever.

His continued silence was getting to her. Why hadn't he disagreed with her comment about Chloe? Since this all began, he'd been a steady stream of reassurances.

Jamie crouched down and gripped her under her armpits. She kept her gaze on his face as he pulled her free, searching— and not finding. When she was kneeling in front of him, she forced herself to put into words the thought that was cutting a hole in her heart. "You think she's dead."

His eyes met hers. They gleamed in the soft glow of the emergency lights. He didn't speak, but his silence told her everything. Everything she'd hoped never to hear. A shudder tore through her. Her teeth started to chatter and great sobs wracked her body. Jamie pulled her against his warm chest and wrapped his strong arms around her, his face buried in her hair.

"She's not dead," he murmured. "I'd know if she were. I'd feel it in my heart."

She wished she could believe him—she needed to believe him. Her heart burned, torn in two. They'd had so little time together, so little time with their daughter. And now it was too late. With that last thought, she slumped against him. She'd have fallen if he hadn't been holding her so tightly.

Through her cries, she heard his radio crackle and Dani say the three sweetest syllables: "I've found her."

CHAPTER 4

Jamie leaned back and ducked his head, turning slightly away from Rickie before speaking into the two-way. "Is she...?" His voice broke and he clamped his mouth shut.

"I can't get to her. I'm sending Coco in with a headset. If she's conscious, maybe we can talk to her. Let her know we're coming," Dani said.

He swallowed and forced himself to keep his hopes in check. "Keep me posted. Rickie's free now. I'll be there in a couple minutes."

Rickie pulled on the sleeve of his turnout coat. "How is Chloe? What did Dani say?"

"She's located her but can't reach her yet. Let's get you outside and then I'll go help Dani."

A cloud descended over her features. Her eyes shot sparks and her hands went to her hips. As usual, his beautiful wife was preparing a mutiny. He held up a hand to stop her, but she wasn't having any of it.

"Jamie Caldwell, you're crazy if you think I'm leaving without my daughter."

Christ he missed her, missed the gentleness of her touch, the softness of her skin. His body tightened at the memories. Shit. This was not the time and place to indulge his fantasies.

Just one touch.

Giving in, he stretched out his hand to stroke her face, but she swatted it aside and flinched when her injured arm collided with his wrist. He dropped his hand and shook his head. What had he been thinking? That everything was forgiven and forgotten because he'd pulled her out from under a wall? Well, yeah. "Babe, listen. You're just going to get in the way."

She leaned forward, her features hard. "I'm. Not. Leaving."

"You can trust me with this. I'll get Chloe out of here even if I die trying."

Her breasts lifted as she blew out a sigh. "There you go again with this trust thing. What is your problem?"

"I know you don't trust me, and a part of me doesn't blame you." He sat her down on the cement block and opened the small first aid kit he'd brought up.

When he swiped the antiseptic over the cut on her wrist, she winced and rubbed her forehead. "Am I hurting you?"

"Not physically." He frowned and she waved her words away with a flick of her hand. "Why do you think I don't trust you?"

He ripped open the packaging of a bandage with a little more force than necessary. The gauze fell to the ground. Cursing, he got another and forced himself to slow down. "Because you never have." When she opened her mouth to speak, he put his fingers against her lips before continuing, his voice rough with pent-up frustration. "After I got back from Indonesia, you stopped trusting me. You wouldn't let me give my daughter a bath. When I tried to feed her, you'd take away the spoon. Later, you wouldn't even let me read her a bedtime story. And now"—he slapped a piece of medical tape over the gauze—"you barely ever let me see her."

"That's not it. We just have a different routine now."

"Now that you're on your own," he finished, stepping back.

She pulled her sleeve over the bandage and kept her eyes lowered. "Yes."

Anger filled his chest. "There isn't room for me in your lives. You've made sure of that."

She dragged her gaze up to his face. "I didn't know you felt this way." She paused and brought a finger to her chin. "Why didn't you ever say anything about it? Oh right." Her voice hardened and she poked her raised finger into his chest.

"Because you were never around long enough."

Jamie grabbed her hand. When she tried to pull it away, he brought it to his lips and kissed her fingers. Rickie was so strong and independent, but the two traits he loved most about her were the very ones keeping them apart. She was right. He hadn't resisted her efforts to neatly package their lives, to make him somewhat extraneous. He hadn't had the heart. He'd watched the worst happen too many times. Watched his fellow firefighters die, and watched their too-dependent wives fall apart and lose themselves, destroying their families. Just like Rickie's mother had.

"If something happens to me, you and Chloe will be fine." Business as usual. He took comfort in that. But what if you don't die, dickhead? You've given up your life, your family, for something that might never happen.

As the words bounced around his head, Rickie pounded her free fist on his chest. Tears spilled from her eyes. "Shut up!" she cried. "Just shut up!"

He knew what this was really about—him dying on the job. He let go of the hand he'd been kissing and gripped her arms. "Calm down, Rickie."

"I don't want to calm down," she sobbed as her fists continued to rain down on him. She wasn't hitting hard enough to hurt him physically, but his heart was breaking.

He pulled her tightly against him, capturing her hands between them. "Shh," he murmured. "Everything will be all right."

He continued to rub comforting circles on her back, but with each passing minute, he believed his reassurances less and less. And that's when he heard the most wonderful sound in the world—his little girl's voice. "Daddy? Daddy? Are you there?"

His heart thrashing in his chest, he let go of Rickie and stood before he pressed the talk button. His throat constricted and he had to push past the tightness. "Chloe, baby. It's Daddy. Are you hurt?"

"I-I'm scared," she hiccuped, her voice raw from crying.

Rickie listened, her face ashen.

"I know, baby. We're coming to get you. It won't be long now. Are you hurt? Daddy needs to know."

"I have a booboo on my legs. Like Bugsy."

Bugsy? With the mic muted, he asked Rickie, "What's Bugsy and what happened to its legs?"

"Her pet guinea pig. She named it after the one in *Bedtime Stories*."

"I didn't know she had a guinea pig."

"That's because she didn't have it for long. She and her friend Nancy were playing with it. A big book fell on it and its leg was crushed. I took it to the vet, but there was nothing to do."

Okay, this was not good news. His daughter's legs were trapped. He could only hope they weren't crushed as well.

Forcing a light tone into his voice, he clicked the two-way back on. "Baby, did something fall on your legs?"

"Uh-huh."

"Can you tell me what it is?"

"No. Mommy's going to be mad."

He narrowed his eyes at Rickie. "I promise you, Chloe. Mommy will *not* be mad. Go on. Tell me."

"Mommy told me to stay with her, but I wanted to see what was in the candy machine."

Oh Christ. "Did the vending machine fall on you, baby?"

Rickie gasped and clutched his wrist, her nails digging into his skin.

"Yes," Chloe wailed.

His stomach burned like he'd swallowed battery acid. Chloe should have never even been here. She should have been at home with him watching *The Little Mermaid*. Instead, she was lying under a goddamn five-hundred-pound vending machine, and he couldn't even get to her.

Beads of sweat dripped down his spine and the sides of his face. His turnout coat was meant to keep fire away, but it wasn't much use when the flames were inside him. "Can you move your legs or your toes, Chloe?"

"Where's Mommy? I want Mommy," she choked through her sobs.

Rickie grabbed his arm and pulled herself up so she could speak into the two-way. "I'm right here, sweetheart. Mommy's right here."

"I'm sorry, Mommy."

"Shh. It's okay. We'll get you out."

Rickie's chest pressed against Jamie's arm as she took a deep shuddering breath, her eyes piercing his. He wrapped his arm around her waist and mouthed, "I promise."

When she laid her head on his shoulder, Jamie took back control of the two-way. He had to know how serious the situation was. "Do your legs hurt, Chloe?"

"They used to. Now I don't feel them."

Biting on his knuckles to keep from roaring, he prayed Dani was already working on getting through the debris. "We're coming to get you. Don't worry. You're going to be fine."

"Okay, Daddy." She sniffled some more and over the air he heard Coco yip. Good. The dog would keep her company and keep her from worrying.

A huge weight took residence on his shoulders as he released the talk button, cutting the connection to Chloe. Rickie stepped out of his embrace and shoved him hard, her eyes glassy with tears. "This is all your fault, James Caldwell. You're the reason our baby's life is in danger. If she didn't need you, I'd kick your ass."

He ducked his head. "You don't think I want to kick my own ass?" For all they knew, his baby's legs could be broken, or worse—she could be paralyzed. At the thought, his chest tightened and his eyes burned. *Christ almighty.* If there was ever a time for prayer, this was it.

The sensation of Rickie's soft palm on his cheek undid him. "Jamie. Hey, I'm sorry. I didn't mean that."

His breath hitched and his shoulders shook with the effort to keep his emotions in check. He was in charge. He was the leader. He had to be strong, or he'd never earn Rickie's trust back. "Yes, you did. And you're right. If I could, I'd change places with her right now."

Stepping closer, she hugged him. "I know you would. I never doubted your love for Chloe."

No. She just doubted his love for *her*. But that was a problem for another day. He cradled her face in his hands and peered deep into her eyes. "I will get our daughter back. If nothing else, trust that."

Looking contrite, she nodded numbly and watched as he

collected his equipment.

When he was done, he took her hand. "Come on, let's go rescue our daughter."

ᔡ 🚂 ᔢ

Strength and determination radiated from Jamie as he led her through what remained of the common area. Dust clogged the air and darkness surrounded them except for the narrow beam from Jamie's flashlight.

In a way, Erica was relieved that the man she'd met and fallen in love with was back. Nothing would keep him from saving Chloe. But this man also terrified her. They were getting a divorce. As soon as Jamie signed the papers, it was a done deal. This wasn't the time for her to waffle. This wasn't the time for her heart to whisper about possible mistakes. Because she wasn't making a mistake. She loved Jamie, every inch of him, with every inch of herself. He was the only one for her. No other man would ever take his place. She knew that like she knew her own name. But she and Jamie were oil and water. They'd never mix together. Not the way they needed to.

"Dani," Jamie called out, startling Erica. She'd been so focused on him, she hadn't even noticed the beams of light a few yards away.

The beams turned and landed on her and Jamie like the king and queen at a prom dance. She shook her head at her own tunnel vision. What was wrong with her? God, she hoped it was just nerves.

"Good to see you safe, Erica," Hollywood said.

"Yeah, glad you're okay." Dani said the words, but her eyes went from their locked hands to Jamie's face. Jamie just stared back.

Hollywood coughed. "Right. K9, normally I'd advise you to go in with the diamond chain saw, even though it weighs almost as much as you do." He paused while she snorted. "But since we don't have power, you'll have to make do with the cordless cutting edge saw. Take the pick axe and bolt cutters, as well as this pry bar. You'll need it to lever the vending machine."

"Thanks," she said, hooking the items into her belt.

"Why is Dani going in?" Erica asked. Surely one of the bigger men would be better suited for the task. "How's she going to get the machine off my little girl?"

Jamie set his equipment down. He looked like he was about to answer, but Dani cut him off, her eyes narrowing on Erica. "Because where Chloe is located is virtually impenetrable for anyone bigger than Coco. As it is, I'm going to have to cut through quite a lot of obstacles just to get to her. And these guys"—she waved her hand around—"would get stuck. And then we'd have another problem on our hands. As for getting the machine off her, I have the same training they have. I will bring your daughter out."

All right then. This obviously wasn't the first time Dani's abilities had been questioned. "Thank you," Erica said.

Dani nodded then grabbed a strap and wound her arms through it so it rested under her breasts.

Erica followed the strap to its end. Her breath caught when she saw the long bright orange board with black tie straps. "Oh God," she cried, pressing her hand to her mouth. "What's that for?"

"It's a spine board," Dani explained without looking at her.

Hearing her gasp, Jamie's arm snaked around Erica's waist and yanked her to his side. "It's just a precaution, honey. If Chloe can crawl, Dani will let her come out on her own."

"And if she can't?"

"If she can't, Dani will pull her out."

She rested her head on Jamie's arm and together they watched her husband's date wind her way through a mountain of wood, plaster, concrete, and metal to save their only child. What a damn nightmare.

Hollywood came to stand beside them. "Don't worry, Erica. Dani's the best."

Jamie pressed his two-way. "Status."

Erica leaned in close so she could hear.

"Hit a sheet of drywall. No way around. I'm using my blade to cut through," Dani said between breaths. "Should be done in a minute."

Soon after, they heard a bang and a crack followed by a "Hot dog!" After a grunt, Dani continued. "Okay, LJ. I'm on the move." They heard more noise as she tossed smaller objects out of her way.

"Careful, Dani," Jamie warned. "We don't want this pile of crap coming down on you."

"I always am, LJ. You know that." Dani laughed and the sound made Erica grit her teeth. She could just imagine what else the woman was always careful about. She pushed away from Jamie's side, sick at the thought that the woman her husband was sleeping with was saving her daughter's life. Unfortunately, when she stepped back she tripped and fell smack against Hollywood. An arm as hard as iron snapped around her waist, pulling her firmly against the man's granite-like chest.

His low laugh rumbled against her back as he leaned down and whispered, "Anytime you want to make him jealous, let me know. But this probably isn't the best time."

She shrugged out of his hold and turned her head to give him a piece of her mind. Hollywood grinned widely, his gaze flicking to Jamie. And oh, boy! If making him jealous had been her goal, she'd have succeeded. Jamie's eyes burned with possessiveness and his body seemed impossibly large as he advanced on her.

"Let go of my wife," he said, his voice a low, dangerous growl.

Hollywood raised his hands in surrender. "My bad," he said, the amusement dancing in his words making it clear he meant the opposite.

"Damn," Dani said, loud enough for Erica to hear her through both men's two-ways.

Jamie gave her one last hard look before turning in the direction Dani had gone. "What is it?" he asked.

"Rebar."

"Fuck. Can you get around it?"

"Not around, not over, not under. I'm going to have to go through it."

"What's your plan?"

Jamie's technical rescue team had some amazing tools, but how could Dani get through reinforced concrete? Erica listened anxiously to Dani's answer.

"It's a support column about fifteen feet long and four feet high by four feet deep. A chunk of cement from the center has already broken out and there are cracks extending out from there for about a foot on each side. If I can chip out the concrete, I can cut the rebar. The hole will be big enough to get the board through."

Visions of the column caving in on Dani and stranding Chloe alone on the other side made Erica sway. She grabbed Jamie's sleeve. When he looked down at her, his brow arched, she asked, "Will it hold after she cuts through it?"

He nodded. "She'll leave enough of the original structure on either side and above the hole to maintain the integrity of the column."

Releasing his arm, she breathed deeply and stepped back.

"Okay, do it," Jamie said to Dani.

"Roger that, LJ."

Dani gave them status updates as she loosened the concrete along the crack and cut several of the steel bars. "I need to do one more layer and then I should be good."

"Make sure there's enough space for an occupied board."

At the sound of Jamie's strangled voice, Erica looked up at him. His eyes were closed and a muscle jumped in his jaw. Her heart clenched with fear. He didn't think Chloe would be able to walk out. She must have whimpered because his eyes shot open and his gaze flew to hers. He didn't say a word, simply brushed his fingers along her cheek. But his eyes spoke of fear and regret.

"Hey, Jamie."

Erica looked up to see Drew and three other men approaching them, boots clomping over the debris, their heavy equipment jiggling and jangling. How such big men could move so fluidly with the amount of gear they carried amazed her. And their arrival thrilled her. Surely with the whole team here, they'd have Chloe out in no time.

"Erica, thank God you're okay." Drew grabbed her in a great bear hug.

She hugged him back, smiling. Of all Jamie's brothers, Drew had always been her favorite. "You should probably thank Jamie instead. He's the one who got me out from under the wall."

Drew stepped back and clapped Jamie on the shoulder. "Nah. They're one and the same."

Jamie pulled him into a chokehold, knocking his helmet off, then he rubbed the top of his brother's head with his knuckles. "Smartass."

Drew laughed, and all the men, including Jamie, joined in.

She'd often wondered why people joked in tense situations like this one. From an outsider's perspective, it had always seemed out of place to her. But now that she was here, in the middle of everything, she understood. When faced with the choice between laughing or crying to relieve the stress of a dangerous situation, laughter was easier to handle.

A sense of hope filled Erica's heart. She'd have her baby in her arms soon. Safe and sound.

Suddenly, everyone stopped, their expressions intent as they listened to someone speaking over the radio. Jamie unclipped the radio from his jacket and held it to his ear. She inched closer to him to hear better, but he shook his head and pulled away. "How bad is it?" he asked.

Her heart started a manic beat against her ribs. Oh God. Had something happened to Chloe? Her hands curled around Jamie's arm as she tried to climb higher. Drew gently disengaged her fingers from Jamie's turnout coat. When she lowered herself to the ground and stepped back, he put an arm around her shoulders and lightly squeezed her bicep.

"What's going on, Drew?"

A look passed between the two brothers. "Get her out of here," Jamie grunted.

What? "I'm not going anywhere. What's wrong, Jamie?" When he remained silent, she insisted. "Tell me. If this concerns Chloe, I have a right to know."

Ignoring her, he flicked his two-way. "Dani, stop all maneuvers until we get a readout."

No! She shrugged Drew's arm off and faced Jamie, desperation making her fierce. "What's the matter with you? You can't just leave our daughter to die under a stupid vending machine."

He narrowed his eyes at her. "I'm not leaving Chloe."

"But you—"

"Just calm down. This isn't helping our daughter. Can't you

40

hear her crying? You're shouting and it's scaring her." He blew out in exasperation. "Give me a minute and I'll explain everything."

Her throat swollen with unspoken questions, she nodded and gave him some space. Surrounded by Jamie's grim-faced team, she waited and listened.

"How much time do we have?" he asked.

All the men swore when the answer came. If someone didn't answer her soon she was going to explode.

Jamie held out his hand. "Come here."

She took it and followed him to where he stopped a few yards away. If something had gone wrong with Chloe, she would... God, she had no idea what she would do. Tears filled her eyes and she searched Jamie's face for answers.

After a few moments, he cleared his throat. "I don't know how to say this."

"J-just say it."

"Okay. The aftershock caused a gas leak. Fumes are filtering up from the basement. We've got about twenty minutes before the levels on this floor become unsafe. We need to evacuate."

CHAPTER 5

Rickie's grip on Jamie's fingers was tight enough to break glass. In that moment, he'd have given anything to turn back the clock. Go back to five forty-five and pick Chloe up from the daycare himself. Go back a year to the day Rickie had sent him packing, the day that would forever be burned into his retinas. Hell, maybe he should go back to the day he'd first met Rickie. Not so he could avoid her, but so he could do everything right. He didn't for one minute regret having had Chloe, but he definitely could have worked on creating a better home for her and on building a stronger marriage with Rickie.

Her bottom lip trembled when she spoke. "What about Chloe?"

He wanted to tell her their daughter would be all right. How could he though? In a matter of minutes, the entire building would be one spark away from a bonfire. "I'll get to her. But you need to leave right now."

The wild shaking of Rickie's head sent her blonde hair whipping around her face. "No. Let me stay, Jamie."

"It's too dangerous." A sound like that of a trapped animal escaped her lips, making his heart break. Christ. Were their positions reversed, he'd want to stay too.

"At least until Dani reaches her. Please, Jamie. I need to stay."

The pain and humility in her tone did him in. Rickie had

never been anything but authoritative and in control. It's what made her so great at her job. "When I say go, you go."

A tremulous smile flashed across her face, gone almost before he noticed it. "Understood."

When they rejoined the group, he asked for an update. "Gas levels?"

"Rising. Seventeen more minutes," Drew said.

"LJ, I've got a problem," Dani interrupted. "I need to use the saw to sever this last piece of rebar."

"No go. Use the bolt cutters."

"Already tried. They aren't big enough."

"Shit." He looked around at the men surrounding him. "If she turns that saw on, the place could blow." One by one, the men nodded. "If anyone wants to leave, go now. No hard feelings." One by one, the men shook their heads.

A lump the size of his fist formed in his throat. He had the best fucking team in the world. "Okay, Dani, do it. But be as quick as you can."

"Got it."

They all held their breaths at the sound of the saw powering up. Jamie held Rickie's hand and wrapped his arm around Drew's shoulders. Prayers from his childhood played in his mind. Was it too obnoxious to ask God for a favor now? He'd never know unless he tried. Bowing his head, he begged God to save his little girl.

Dani's whoop over the radios sounded like a heavenly aria when it came. "I'm through, LJ." Coco's excited barking joined the team's gleeful encouragement. "Coco's here. I told her to stay with Chloe, so I must be very close."

Since he hadn't wanted Chloe to be frightened by the team's radio chatter, he'd asked her to turn off the radio Coco had brought her. But now that his luck seemed to be turning, he wanted to tell his daughter that help was near. "Call to her. Ask her to turn the walkie-talkie on," he said.

A few seconds later, he heard a click and the sweetest softest voice. "Daddy?"

"I'm here, baby."

"Coco was barking. I got scared, but then I heard Dani."

"That's right. Dani's coming to get you. You be a big girl

and do what she says. Okay?"

"Okay. I'm not going to die, am I, Daddy?"

The air left his lungs in one awful whoosh, as though the building had collapsed on his chest. Beside him, Rickie made a small keening sound. "No. Of course not," he said, more vehemently than he should have. Softening his tone, he asked, "Can you see Dani or Coco yet?"

"Coco came back." He heard slurping sounds accompanied by Chloe's giggles.

An ache started deep in his chest. "I love you, baby."

Dani's voice came over the air, calm and light. "I've got her, LJ."

"Good. Turn her radio off." He waited to hear the click, then spoke to Dani. "I'll try to ask questions you can answer without scaring her. What's on her? Is it the vending machine?"

"Yes."

"Can you lift it?"

"Yes."

"Can you pull her out from underneath at the same time?"

"Maybe."

"Too cramped?"

"Time is a bigger issue."

Shit. How could he have forgotten? If he didn't pull it together and keep a cool head, he'd get them all killed. "Levels?" he asked Drew.

"Almost critical. Ten minutes."

"We need to get SCBAs to them," Hollywood said.

"How?" asked Colin. "Dani's the only one who fits, and even that was a tight squeeze."

Jesus Fucking Christ. Had he really thought his luck was changing? He was a goddamn idiot. Now his child and one of his team members were essentially trapped without masks and instead of planning how to get equipment to them, he'd been praying.

"I'll do it."

He heard Rickie's words but couldn't make any sense of them. "Do what?"

"Bring tanks and masks to Dani and Chloe."

"Absolutely not." Civilians did not participate in rescue

missions. Ever.

She rounded on him then, arms on her hips, eyes blazing. "Look, Jamie. I'm the only one who can do it. All of you are too big. I know I can fit; I'm smaller than Dani."

"Honey, you have no training. You'll just get hurt. And those tanks are heavy."

"Don't you 'honey' me, James Caldwell. I'm their only chance, and I'm a hell of a lot stronger than you think." Without looking back, she grabbed his SCBA from the ground and headed the way Dani had gone.

He lunged forward and grabbed her elbow. "At least let us outfit you properly. Evan, give her your trousers and extrication gloves." Given that he was almost a foot taller than his wife and outweighed her by a hundred pounds or so, his own turnout gear would be more hindrance than help.

Drew came up beside him, shrugging out of his jacket. "Take my jacket. With the sleeves rolled up, it should be okay."

Once she was dressed, Jamie helped her adjust the shoulder straps and waist belts of the SCBA, then he took off his helmet and secured it on her head along with the mask. "Click here to turn the radio on and off. There's an amplifier in the helmet."

Hollywood brought over another SCBA. "Try not to bang it around too much."

"Shouldn't I bring two extras?"

Jamie rubbed the back of his neck. Did she think she was Wonder Woman? "Each air cylinder weighs about twenty-five pounds. Think you can get through all that rubble lugging an extra seventy-five pounds?"

She gulped. "We'll share."

"Smart choice." When she turned to leave, he stopped her with a hand on her arm. She looked up and arched a brow. "Turn on the radio now. Dani will talk you through to her location."

Following his earlier instructions, she turned on the radio and started to leave. He stopped her again. She sighed. "Now what?"

"Be careful." He could convince himself he hadn't said the three words he most wanted to say so that he wouldn't upset her right before she started out. But that would be a lie. He hadn't said it because he was a coward. If they were all going to die, he'd rather die with the illusion that had he said those three words, Rickie would have said them back.

ಸಂ 🚇 ೞ

Erica stared into Jamie's eyes, saw fear and resignation. He cared about her. It was obvious from his tone and his expression. But did he love her? Unless she heard the words, she wouldn't know. Too much had happened between them, and she couldn't trust her judgment or her instincts where he was concerned.

She nodded. "I'll follow Dani's instructions to the letter."

Her heart full of words and emotions she'd refused to let out for years, she picked up the second tank and mask and walked over to where she'd first seen Dani enter. "Dani?" she asked, checking to make sure the radio was working.

"Right here, Erica."

"I'm at the spot where you started—the big heating duct."

"Okay, you'll need to belly crawl through it. It'll be a tight fit with the SCBA on your back, but you can make it. Push the other tank in front of you."

With careful movements so as not to throw herself off balance, Erica got down on her knees and slid the tank into the duct. The interior was so dark, she needed the flashlight or she'd be fumbling around blindly.

"When you get to the end, the tank will bump into a wall," Dani continued. "You'll have to turn it to your left."

The bulkiness of the unfamiliar clothing made the distance to the other end seem interminable. Because her gloves were too large, she kept dropping the flashlight, and her bunker trousers kept sliding on the slippery material of the duct's surface. Like a child on a Slip 'N Slide, each time she pushed forward with her knees, she'd fall face first. Inch by inch, despite the new set of bruises on her legs, she pressed on and eventually the tank hit an obstacle.

Angling it in the direction Dani had instructed, she edged her way out of the duct only to end up squished between a wall and a downed support beam. God, how did Jamie and his team do this on a daily basis? She took a deep breath.

Suck. Hiss.

The uneven sound of her breathing in the faceplate was overwhelming and made her realize just how vulnerable she was. "I'm out," she said.

Dani must have heard the shakiness in her voice because unlike earlier, her tone was calm and encouraging. "You're doing great, Erica. Walk along the wall and the beam about ten yards until you get to a point where a second beam has fallen over the first. Oh, and lift up the second tank in that area. There's a lot of sharp metal on the ground there."

Wonderful. Erica looked down at her poor abused running shoes. This is when those thick fireman boots come in handy. Too bad she wasn't wearing any. She should be grateful though. There wasn't much room, but at least she could stand and walk more or less normally. Using the light from the helmet, she picked her way along the wall, avoiding whatever metal she managed to see. Unfortunately, the beam from the flashlight was narrow, and she didn't see the jagged edge of the filing cabinet in time. She stifled a scream as it cut through the rubber sole of her sneaker.

"Erica?"

Using the wall for support, she lifted up her foot and shined the light on it to examine the damage. The bottom of her shoe had a big gash in it. At least her foot had been spared. Sort of. Her heel burned and a few drops of blood oozed through the hole in the rubber.

"You okay, Erica?" Dani asked again, sounding anxious.

"Nothing I can't handle." She'd suffer through this and much worse for her daughter. Cautiously, she started walking again, following Dani's instructions.

After a few moments, Dani broke the silence. "So, how are things going with you and Jamie?"

Suck. Hiss.

Adrenaline surged through Erica's system at the question. It was bad enough her life and her daughter's depended on this woman. Did Dani have to rub in the fact that she was Jamie's girlfriend as well? Gritting her teeth, she spat out, "Seeing as how he's dating you, I'm sure you know exactly how well things are going." *Bitch.*

Dani laughed. Laughed!

Erica forced her feet to keep moving, reminding herself that Chloe—not Jamie or his other relationships—was the only thing that mattered. When she reached the overlapping beams, she reined in her anger and said, "I'm there. What now?"

"Crawl over the beams at the point where they intersect, then go right about forty-five degrees. If you're in the right place, in six yards, you should reach the failed support column I cut through."

Erica examined the beams, trying to figure out how she was going to get over their combined height. The beams reached her shoulders and without footholds or something to step on, there was no way she could pull herself and the extra fifty pounds of tanks she was carrying over. Despair dug serrated claws into her heart. Maybe Jamie was right. Maybe she'd let her pride override her abilities. She wasn't trained and she had no idea what to do. Inhaling deeply, she fought back the tears burning her eyes.

"Find something you can stand on to help you over," Dani added gently.

Why hadn't she thought of that? Mustering up her courage, she searched the nearby debris and located several large blocks of cement and some wooden planks.

"We're not dating, you know."

Erica paused in the act of organizing her findings into a table of sorts. "Jamie cancelled his evening with Chloe because he was going out with you. He told me himself."

"Well, he lied then," Dani said.

"Why would he do that?" Erica finished building her platform and tested it with one foot. A little wobbly, but it would have to do.

"To make you jealous, maybe?"

Standing on the platform, she lifted the second tank on top of the beams and settled it in the space between them. Then she hoisted herself up, pulling with all the strength in her arms. But the weight of the tank on her back dragged her back down. While one foot landed squarely on the platform, the injured one slipped off the edge. "Ow!"

"Everything okay over there?" Dani asked, her voice anxious.

Ignoring the woman's question, Erica asked one of her own as she massaged her ankle. Boots were definitely non-optional when traipsing through a minefield of obstacles as dangerous as this one. "Why should I believe you?"

"I'm not interested in Jamie."

That drew her up short. "Why not?" Erica blurted before she could stop herself. The man was gorgeous, smart, and made good money. Any woman in her right mind would want Jamie. *So why don't you?*

Thankfully, Dani's response meant she could avoid her own question. "I'm in love with his brother."

"Drew?" she asked, unable to keep the incredulity from her voice. Two firefighters getting involved would be a disaster. She bounced with her knees and stretched her arms as far as she could, then jumped. Her hands hooked on the far beam. Swinging her feet to the side, she anchored one leg over the first beam. Tightening all her muscles, she pulled herself up and flattened herself on the beam to keep from falling.

Suck. Hiss.

Sweat streamed down her back between her shoulder blades. The temperature inside her turnout coat had to be at least one hundred and ten degrees. No wonder Jamie and his team didn't have an ounce of fat on them.

Dani's laughter rang out. "No way. Drew's like a brother to me. I meant Will."

Was it some sort of firefighter rule that they had to shorten everyone's name? "Does Jamie know?" Since the separation, Jamie had been living with William. Maybe Dani had been using one brother to get the other.

"Yes. He's been helping me out."

"Really?" Having regained her breath, Erica twisted her hips until she was aligned with the V of the intersecting wooden beams and let herself slide down, pulling the extra tank after her. Once her feet hit the ground with a solid painful thump, she scanned the area and identified the forty-five degree direction. Her limping steps were about half a yard each, so twelve or so should get her to the support column.

Dani sighed. "Jamie keeps finding excuses to invite me over. But Will has no idea I'm alive. As far as he's concerned, I'm just one of Jamie's work buddies."

Erica wasn't surprised. Of all the Caldwell brothers, William—the accountant—was the least likely to go for a tomboy like Dani. He harked back so thoroughly to the Caldwell's aristocratic British forebears that he should have an accent. If William even owned a pair of jeans, Erica would be truly shocked. "Good luck with that one. Okay, I've reached the cement beam."

"Push the spare tank through first, then follow. The hole is about two feet high and it might be a bit of a tight fit. When you reach the other side, go straight about ten feet until you reach a pile of junk."

A pile of junk? Okay. Shoving the tank in ahead of her, she concentrated on squeezing herself and the tank on her back into the two-foot hole. Once again she was entombed in complete inky darkness, save for the glow from her flashlight.

Suck. Hiss.

The sound of her breathing added to the creepiness of the cave-like hole. Her chest tightened, making it hard to squeeze air into her compressed lungs. All she needed now was to have a panic attack and get stuck here. Everyone she cared about would die.

"I walked in on Jamie today, sitting at the table in the lunchroom, staring at the divorce papers."

Dani must have noticed the change in her breathing. Erica laid her head on her arm, gripping the flashlight and the extra tank, while attempting to calm herself. "He told me he lost them."

"I don't think he wants to sign."

The cement was rough, with sharp edges that tugged at her trousers. The suspenders kept them from being pulled off, but the Velcro straps around her ankles did nothing to keep them from riding up her legs, exposing her skin. The jacket scrunched up under her arms and the sleeves pushed up to her elbows. Jagged cement tips tore through her turnout gear and scraped her lower legs, forearms, and belly. It felt like she was being dragged over a cheese grater, and each new cut stung as fresh sweat dripped into it. Nothing in her life had prepared her for this.

If Dani's goal with this conversation was to distract her from her mounting anxiety, it was working. "What makes you say that?" she asked, pushing with her feet to inch herself forward. Dust rose up and coated her facemask, blinding her. She stilled and wiped a gloved hand across it, listening, waiting for Dani's response.

"I figure if he'd wanted to sign them, he'd have done so already. When a guy wants free of the ball and chain, it doesn't take him three months to autograph a few sheets of paper."

Her stomach clenched—whether with hope or fear, she wasn't certain. Why hadn't Jamie said anything to her? When they'd met with their lawyers, he'd agreed to everything. She'd expected—hoped—he'd put up some sort of fight.

"So you want this divorce?" Dani asked.

As Erica reached for the spare tank, her sleeve snagged on a piece of rebar that stuck out from the cement. She tried to jiggle it free, but the metal was anchored deep. "That's not what I said."

"Maybe not, but that's what it sounds like."

"What do you mean?" Frustrated with her inability to free her sleeve as much as with Dani's comments, she yanked her arm as hard as she could and ripped the turnout jacket free. With her elbows, she hitched herself forward like a caterpillar until the hole narrowed and the tank on her back screeched against the cement. She rolled onto her side so there'd be more room for the tank, and with her feet anchored as best she could with her running shoes, she wiggled her hips and propelled herself forward. Soon the spare tank started to tip over the edge. Holding tightly, she slowly lowered it to the ground. Dani's answer came as Erica crawled out from inside the concrete support beam.

"Seems to me you've done everything possible to shove Jamie out of your life. Out of his daughter's life."

"It's what he wants."

"You sure about that?"

Something inside compelled her to give voice to her deepest concerns. But was Dani the right person to confide in? "There's no guarantee he'd be around anyway."

"What?"

"Isn't this situation answer enough? Jamie could be killed at any time."

"Look where you are, Erica. Right now, you're in more danger than he is. *Anyone* can die at any time."

There was a silence over the radio, but she had nothing to say. Her own father, an elementary school teacher, had died on his way home from work, killed by a drunk driver. There were no guarantees for any of them.

"But you know what, Erica?"

"What?"

"If you push him away now, he might as well be dead."

Suck. Hiss.

Oh God. She was such an idiot. She'd been so determined not to depend on Jamie, so determined to prove that she could raise her daughter alone, so determined not to be her mother, that she'd erased Jamie from their lives, depriving herself of a wonderful husband, and depriving her daughter of a loving father.

Assuming they survived this night, and assuming he still loved her, did their marriage even stand a chance? If they worked at it, could it survive as well?

Qué será, será. She couldn't dwell on this now. The only thing she needed to focus on was saving their daughter. She'd reached the pile of junk. "I'm at the pile. Where do I go from here?"

"Unfortunately, you're going to have to crawl over it."

Misgiving tightened her chest as she looked from her sneaker-clad feet to the mound of rubble. Steeling her spine, she cradled the spare tank in her arm and placed her foot on a sturdy-looking block. She pushed herself up, careful to keep her balance. After cresting the pile, she slid one foot forward until it caught on a piece of wood. She nudged it to see if it would hold and huffed out a breath when it did. She could do this. She would.

Like a tightrope walker, she held her free arm out and took a step. Her foot sank into the debris, pitching her forward. Everything happened in a flash. Within seconds, her body slammed into the ground, knocking the breath from her lungs.

She sucked in great gulps of air, stopping only when she

began to feel lightheaded. On the verge of hyperventilation, she strained against the weight of the SCBA on her back and reached for the flashlight that had fallen a few feet away. Her only thought was to get on her feet. Time was running out.

Feeling like an astronaut in the heavy, bulky suit, she pulled her knees under her chest to give herself leverage. Pain stabbed in her thigh.

Muffling a cry, she rolled onto her butt and looked down to see a jagged piece of glass sticking out from her leg. With shaking fingers, she reached down and yanked it out. Drops of blood clung to the dirty glass. Nausea filled her throat. Almost desperately, she ripped open the mask's faceplate. All she needed now was to drown in her own vomit. Again and again, she swallowed and took shallow breaths through her nose.

She stared up into the darkness of what had been her workplace, and tears filled her eyes. Why had she thought she could do this?

She was going to let everyone down.

She was just like her mother.

CHAPTER 6

Jamie heard his wife's soft sobs through the radio, each one gouging his heart. Christ, sending Rickie in had been a big fucking mistake. But what choice had he had? She was their only hope for getting the SCBA to Chloe and Dani. And without her, Dani couldn't free Chloe from the vending machine. This rescue was turning into a major clusterfuck with the strongest members of the team standing around waiting, feeling like dumbasses. His years of experience meant nothing today. All he could do was help Rickie through this.

"Come on, babe. You can do this. Take a deep breath and tell me what happened."

He heard a gasp, then Rickie's shocked voice. "J-Jamie?"

"Yeah, it's me. What's wrong?"

"I fell and cut my thigh."

Shit. "Are you bleeding?" If she'd hit an artery, he'd have to blast his way to her. And risk blowing them all up in the process.

"Some."

Air rushed out of his lungs as relief threatened to overwhelm him. Still, better safe than sorry. "Use one of the straps we used to secure the pant legs around your ankles. Tie it as tightly as possible around your thigh above the cut. Can you do that, honey?"

He heard rustling sounds as she moved around.

"Done. Thank you, Jamie."

"For what?"

"For being there."

Always. She just didn't believe it yet. Unless Dani's words had sunk in. It'd been hard staying silent while Dani had been talking to Rickie about the divorce papers. But something had told him to stay out of it.

"You ready to keep going?" he asked, his tone unhurried. He didn't want to frighten her, but they were running out of time. The gas fumes would soon be reaching critical levels and not only was the risk of explosion very high, but Dani and Chloe were inhaling toxic air with every breath.

"I'm good. What do I do now?"

Dani's voice came on the line, cool and calm. "You're almost here, Erica. But this last part's a bit tricky. Ten yards to your left is a cement wall about five feet high. Jamie, did you give Erica the climbing rope?"

"Rickie, look at your belt. Attached on your right side is a rope. On one end is a grappling hook. You'll need to rotate the latch mechanism at the top a quarter turn. Once the claws pop out, rotate the latch another quarter turn to lock it in place. Then swing the hook over the wall. Can you do that?"

He heard her harsh breaths as she threw the rope, followed by a clunk as the claws hit the cement. "How do I get it to hook onto something?" she asked.

"Gently pull on the rope. As the hook moves up the wall, the claws should sink into a soft spot or a crevice."

"Oh! I think it worked."

A smile tugged at his lips. "Now give it a sharp yank to make sure it holds."

"Crap, it came all the way over."

"Stay calm and try it again. Throw the hook over the wall, then slowly pull it back."

A few seconds later, he heard her sigh. "I think I've got it now."

"Great. Do you remember that time we went mountain climbing and we had to go up a part that was pretty steep? It's just like that. Walk up the wall." That day would be forever etched in his mind as one of the happiest of his life. Rickie had finally agreed to go hiking with him. They'd climbed up the mountain and had a picnic near the top. For dessert, they'd had each other.

His body tightened as he remembered the softness of her skin warmed by the sun, the scent of her hair, the glorious feeling of slipping inside her. *Mind on the job, asshole.* "You can do this, Rickie."

"I'm glad you're so confident, Jamie," she said, her voice tinted with sarcasm.

"Chloe's counting on you. We both are."

"No pressure. Thanks."

He chuckled at her acerbic tone. "Rickie, you're the most capable, independent woman I've ever known. You can do anything you want."

She scoffed. "Whatever. Here goes nothing."

He listened attentively as she climbed the wall, the extra weight of the two oxygen units making her strain and grunt. "That's it, honey. Slow and easy."

When all he heard was her rasping breath, he knew she'd reached the top of the wall. "I bet you're wondering how you get down now."

"Something like that," she said between pants.

Dani broke in. "I left my rope in place. Look around. You'll see it."

"I see it," Rickie said even as he heard her move toward it. More shuffling, and then she said, "I'm down."

"I'm sending Coco to you. Just follow her. You'll be here in a minute," Dani said.

Jamie heard Coco's happy barking as she found Rickie. From her rapid breathing, he knew she was on the move again, following the dog to their daughter. His chest filled with warmth. Maybe they'd all survive this nightmare after all. Thanks to his courageous wife. "You're wrong, you know," he said softly, ignoring the fact that Dani and the entire team were listening in.

"About what?" Rickie asked, sounding guarded.

"I don't want the divorce." He had to tell her the truth. Make her understand. "I've wanted you from the moment I laid eyes on you at that party. I love our daughter and our family."

"Then why did you back out?"

Her angry words lashed at him. He could understand now how she could have misinterpreted his actions and intentions. "I knew you were afraid. That if I died on the job, you'd be left struggling like your mom."

"So what? You wanted me to be *prepared?*"

"I gave you the space I thought you needed."

"Ha! I didn't need *space*, I needed a husband. One who was there."

"Rickie, be honest with yourself. You pushed me so far away, I live in a different zip code."

But then she screamed and he heard scraping sounds, followed by a loud crash. Panic consumed him. "Rickie!"

"I-I'm okay. My shoe slipped and I tripped."

Running shoes were a damn sight better than the high heels she usually wore, but it was a wonder she hadn't lost her footing before. "Are you hurt?"

Her breathing sped up as she struggled to get back on her feet, the erratic hissing coming through the radio loud and clear. With each ragged inhale, his guilt increased. "Rickie, tell me if you're hurt," he said again.

"I'm just so tired of fighting with you, Jamie." Her voice hitched and he knew then and there that she still cared.

"I want things to be good between us again, babe. I miss you."

She laughed, the sound bitter. "When were things *good*, Jamie? When you married me out of an archaic sense of obligation?"

He gritted his teeth. Why couldn't she believe he'd married her because he loved her? "I wanted you."

"But did you love me? Did you ever love me, Jamie?"

"You know I did. I *do*. When Chloe was born, I thought I had it all. That if I died then, I'd die happy."

"And I'd have been left alone, a single mother with a fatherless child."

He remained silent for a moment, letting her words sink in. Finally, he cleared his throat. "Isn't that what you and Chloe are now?"

Coco's sharp barks and his wife's soft sob reached his ears.

"I'm not dead, Rickie. You're afraid of something that might never happen. You can't live life this way, never being happy, never letting your guard down because you're protecting yourself from anything that can go wrong."

"I can't be like you, Jamie. You never worry about anything."

"I'm worried about all of us right now." The lives of his family and his team were all on the line. And their chances of surviving diminished with each passing minute.

ॐ ☃ ☙

"Mommy! Mommy!"

The mix of pain, fear, and elation in her daughter's cry had Erica's body rushing with adrenaline. Ripping off her gloves, she knelt beside Chloe and began to gently feel her for injuries. "I'm here, sweetie. We're going to get you out," she said, turning to Dani with an expectant look.

Dani had already begun building a crib at the base of the vending machine. Erica estimated she'd already raised it three inches. Beads of perspiration rolled down her cheeks and her breathing was labored. Grabbing the second SCBA, Erica brought it to Dani. "You look like you could use some fresh air," she said so as not to alarm her daughter, who was looking on with large frightened eyes.

Nodding her thanks, Dani slipped the straps onto her shoulders and placed the mask over her face. For several moments, she did nothing but inhale deeply. Rickie hurried back to Chloe and transferred her own mask to her daughter's face. "Breathe slow and deep."

"While I raise this a couple more inches, can you arrange the stretcher so when you pull her out, she slides onto it?" Dani asked.

The void was small and cave-like. The panel of sheetrock above them had probably protected Chloe from some of the smaller, but no less deadly, debris that had fallen from the ceiling. Carefully, Erica cleared some space for the stretcher, placing the foot of it at Chloe's head. When she was done, she explained to Chloe what they were going to do, then took the mask back for a few fortifying gulps of air. After replacing the mask on Chloe's face, she gave Dani a thumbs up.

"Ladies, how's everything going?"

Jamie's confident voice settled her jumpy stomach. And her daughter's smile made her heart squeeze. If nothing else, she had to acknowledge that Jamie did love his daughter.

"Daddy! Mommy's here. She brought me a special mask."

"A special mask for my special girl," he said, and she could hear the amusement in his words. "Be sure to share with Mommy. She's pretty special too."

Her daughter laughed and for a moment, Erica imagined how happy they might be again if she and Jamie could get past this mountain in their path. But what if they couldn't? What if the wall between them was too high? The thought brought tears to her eyes.

"Erica?"

Dani touched her arm, and the worry in her eyes brought Erica back to the present. Back to the nightmare they were living. "Sorry. I'm okay."

"Good." Dani moved to the far side of the vending machine and grabbed the pole she was using as a lever. "When I say go, start pulling her out, very slowly. Once she's clear, let me know."

Erica grabbed Chloe under the arms and waited. Slowly, Dani pushed on the lever and the vending machine rose another inch. "Go," Dani said.

On her signal, Erica slowly tugged her daughter out from under the machine. Her gaze shot to Chloe's legs and a jolt stiffened her shoulders. The sharp edge of a bone was visible through the thin blood-soaked material of Chloe's cotton pants. Her little face scrunched in pain as Erica slid her onto the stretcher until her head rested on the neck support, but she didn't utter a single sound. Brave, just like her father. "Clear."

"Okay, now move the stretcher back a foot or two, as much as you have room for."

Erica maneuvered her daughter to safety and stroked her hair. Earlier Chloe had said she couldn't feel either of her legs. Hopefully, they'd just gone numb. "How are your legs, sweetie?"

"They hurt," she said, her voice thin, frightened.

"Both of them?"

Chloe's lip jutted out and her eyes welled.

"Shh, it's okay," Erica murmured, running her finger along Chloe's cheek. She didn't like her daughter being in pain, but it meant she wasn't paralyzed, and for that Erica was very grateful. "We'll be out of here soon."

Dani lowered the vending machine back onto the cribbing and released the lever. Her shoulders slumped and she inhaled deeply before speaking into her radio. "She's clear, Jamie."

Whoops of joy filled Erica's ears as everyone on the team congratulated them. "Did you hear that, baby girl?" Jamie said to Chloe.

"Am I going to be alright, Daddy?"

"You bet. Mommy and Dani are superheroes today."

"Like Wonder Woman?"

"Exactly like that. Okay, ladies. Are you ready for the trip back? The sooner we all get out of here the better."

Erica looked at Dani, who smiled. "Yep, we're heading back right now."

Dani crouched beside the stretcher and strapped Chloe into place. "Okay, kiddo. There might be some bumps, and you might feel like you're falling sometimes, but trust us, okay? We'll be out of here in no time."

Her lips pressed tightly together, Chloe nodded to Dani. Erica gently squeezed her daughter's hand then took another few gulps of air from the mask before giving it back to Chloe.

"From here on out, you share with me," Dani said. "I'm going to take the lead. When I get tired, we'll switch. You watch and help keep things stable."

"Okay," Erica said, moving to the foot of the stretcher.

Just as Dani began pulling the stretcher out of the small void, Coco bounded up to Dani, barking and pressing herself against the woman's side. "What's wrong, girl?" Dani asked, smoothing her hands over the dog's back. Coco howled and even from where she stood, Erica could see the dog's body tremble.

"Oh, shit!" Dani shouted, crouching over Chloe's face. "Get down, Erica. Cover your head with your arms."

The floor swayed as a powerful aftershock ripped through the building. Cracking and crashing filled the air as the already damaged building crumbled. Erica edged her way closer to

Chloe and touched her leg, determined to be with her daughter in their last moments. She didn't have the oxygen mask on, but she did have the radio clipped to her turnout jacket. Pressing the button, she shouted, "Be safe, Jamie." *Come on, Erica. This might be your last chance.* "I love you."

As the words left her mouth, something enormous crashed on top of them. She couldn't hold back her shrieks as what looked like a steel I-beam cut through the sheetrock above her. It crashed onto the vending machine, partially embedded in the machine's frame. Would it stop there or crush them all? She had no way of knowing.

Lightly squeezing Chloe's leg, she prayed Jamie had heard her final words.

CHAPTER 7

Jamie and his team dropped to one knee as a violent aftershock shook the building. Time seemed to slow and Jamie's attention was drawn to a crack in the ceiling. *Christ, no!*

They were so close to victory. Let him be wrong.

The groaning of the building as it swayed was so loud, he almost missed his wife's frantic words over the radio. "Be safe, Jamie."

"Rickie, are you all right?"

He watched, his limbs paralyzed by horror, as a massive concrete support column from the north side of the building buckled. The I-beam it was holding up toppled with it, crashing down directly over the location of his wife and child.

Her loud scream filled his faceplate, and he knew he'd hear it until the day he died.

The connecting wall and ceiling crumbled and thousands of pounds of construction material pounded down over the area in the beam's wake. A roar tore through his throat as he imagined their bodies mangled and trapped under the weight. "Rickie! Chloe!"

When she didn't reply, his heart broke, unable to believe things would end this way. It couldn't be. This couldn't happen.

Then he heard it. So soft, so final. "I love you."

"Rickie!" he screamed again. "Rickie!" *Oh God. No.* Determined to get to her, to Chloe, he took off at a run, charging through the fallen structures.

Until strong arms dragged him back. "Jamie. It's too unstable. Remember your training."

Drew's calm voice pissed him off. "Fuck my training. My family is there. I've got to save them."

"I know. They're my family too. But you can't do it this way."

Jamie looked down at his younger brother. He was solidly built, but not as tall as Jamie. "Who's going to stop me?"

A hand clasped his shoulder. "I will."

His heart sank. If push came to shove, Hollywood could probably take him. Fuck. "Come on, guys. You can't expect me to just stand here and wait for them to die. We're the damn technical rescue team. Let's do our jobs and rescue them."

Hollywood clapped him on the back. "Now you're talking. But we aren't charging in there like jackasses on meth."

Jamie looked around, considering the scene. Going forward was out. The north end was out. His gaze shifted upward to the gaping hole in the ceiling. He pointed. "That's it. I'm going in from the next floor. We'll use a pulley to move the beam."

Drew grabbed him by the neck and pulled his head down until their foreheads met. "I know how upset you are, Jamie. But we don't even know if they're alive."

Jamie shuddered as though he'd been shocked with a Taser. He struggled to pull away, but Drew just held him tighter. He had to make Drew understand. "But we don't know that they're dead either."

"Finally, a believer."

Dani's annoyed voice sounded like the singing of angels in that moment.

"Dani! Is everyone all right?" His stomach churned as he awaited her answer.

"A little shaken, a little stirred. But we're alive."

His legs wobbled, and he'd have fallen if Hollywood hadn't steadied him.

"Jamie?"

"Erica?" He silently thanked God for giving him another chance.

"Please, don't take any unnecessary risks," she said.

Had she been hit in the head? He'd die to save her and Chloe. "Don't worry about me, babe. Focus on yourself and Chloe. Try to keep her calm. Dani, what's the situation?"

"The machine we all bitched about saved our lives. The I-beam's jacked up against it. But the way out is blocked now. So you guys need to get your fantastic butts over here and get us out," Dani said.

"I second that," Rickie said, and he could hear the smile in her voice.

"I'm working on a plan." A grin ripped across his face. Maybe this time, luck would be on his side. "Okay, guys. Grab your gear and let's head up one floor."

They hauled all their gear up the stairs to the fourth floor and moved into position. Drew came up to him, worry on his face. "What is it?" he asked.

"Gas levels are rising faster. We need to get the security team out."

Jamie's brows furrowed. Fuck. He'd almost forgotten about the gas. He held his hand up and called the men to his side. "Things are getting very dangerous. Any minute, we could have an explosion or a full structural collapse. I know some of you have family and loved ones. Don't risk yours to save mine. Anyone who wants out, you're free to leave now." He met and held their gazes one by one. No one moved.

"No one will ever know," he insisted. Still no one left. "All right then. Let's do this. Colin and Evan, make sure the security guys leave the building. Then come back and be ready to get Chloe and Rickie out of the building." He paused and everyone waited for him to continue. "And call for a back-up medic unit. We're going to need it." The sooner they could get Chloe to the hospital, the better. Rickie's injuries weren't life-threatening, but he'd feel better if she was seen by a doctor. Then there was Dani. God only knew how much of the gas she'd inhaled.

"Right on it, LJ," Colin said as he and Evan headed for the stairwell.

Jamie stepped to the edge of the hole in the floor and looked down at the scene below. The steel I-beam that had nearly destroyed his family was clearly visible. Looking up, he pointed at an exposed area of the ceiling. "Get the rigging in place. One set for me and one set for the beam."

"You should let one of us do it," Gabe said.

He shook his head. "Nope. I have the most experience with rope rescues."

They made quick work of anchoring the ropes on the beams and setting up the pulley systems. Within minutes, Jamie was strapped into a harness and holding onto the simple web sling they'd use to raise the I-beam. They only needed to lift it up a foot or two, just enough for the women to slip out from under the debris and get Chloe's stretcher through. The quake had certainly disturbed things, so their path out might not be as easy as it had been going in. He only hoped they didn't encounter any obstacles that required drilling. With the gas levels so high, it would be suicide to even attempt it.

Hollywood double-checked the threading of the climbing rope through the figure eight descender and its attachment to the carabiner on Jamie's harness. Then he yanked on the ropes to test the strength of the anchor system while all the men held onto the ends of the ropes tug-of-war style. "Okay, LJ. Ready when you are."

Leaving the relative safety of the floor behind, Jamie swung into the void and rappelled down one level, using his hands on the rope to control his rate of descent. Seconds later, his feet touched the ground. "Dani, I'm here. Make sure everyone is in a protected position." When the I-beam lifted, the chances were very high that more shit would fall on them. "But be ready to move when I say go."

"Understood, LJ."

With light movements, he secured the sling around the beam and attached it to the master link at the end of the second rope. After double-checking the equipment, he alerted Hollywood. "Okay, lift it up. Smooth and steady." He kept his hands on the beam to stabilize it as it angled upward, inch by agonizing inch. "Get ready, Dani. A little more, Hollywood."

The large crossbeam they'd used as leverage for the sling creaked and groaned. Jamie jerked his head up, concerned. "Stop. Hollywood, get some binoculars. Check out the leverage pieces."

A few rustlings and curses later, Hollywood said, "We've got trouble. The load is too high and the beam is bending."

"How bad?"

"I'm seeing some edge cracks."

What had he said earlier about his luck holding out? Yeah. He'd fucking jinxed himself. "Well, we can't stop now."

"But if it breaks—"

"I'm well aware. Keep going." Under his hands, the I-beam pinning the women lifted another inch. "Dani? Everyone okay?"

"We're getting some fallout, but nothing too bad."

"Things might get rough, so try to move into position for exit."

He heard some quiet whispers and shuffling. "Need two more inches at least," Dani said.

"You got it." As the beam rose, he added his support beneath it, guiding it with his hands. "Easy does it, Hollywood. Almost there."

"That's good, LJ," Dani said. "We're moving out."

"Try to keep everyone calm and make sure Rickie gets her share of oxygen. Air's real bad."

"Will do. I'll let you know once we're clear."

As he listened to their movements, he heard a sharp snap from above, along with the shouts of his team. "LJ, the cracks are getting larger." Hollywood warned.

Without thought, Jamie moved under the beam, shoring it with his arms and shoulders. He pulled a knife from his belt, flipped it open and cut the ropes holding the beam. The last thing he needed was for the failing beam to fall on their heads. But the weight of the I-beam almost drove him to his knees. "Dani," he panted, widening his stance. "By all that's holy, run like the fucking wind and save my family."

"LJ! What—?"

Hollywood saved him from answering. "Dani, the anchor was about to rupture, so he cut the ropes. Get everyone out of there. Fast."

"Oh God." She didn't say any more to him, but Jamie heard her giving Rickie instructions.

He also heard Rickie's soft cries. He'd forgotten she had a

radio too. His throat felt like a garotte was wrapped around it, but he pushed the words out. He had to say goodbye. "Everything will be all right, Rickie. Just know that I love you and Chloe. I always have. I always will."

"Jamie, no. Don't—"

"It's the only way, Rickie. Please just..." His voice broke and he stopped himself. This was not the time to be morbid. *Don't let our daughter forget me.* Sucking the words and thoughts down, he walled them off in a secret corner of his heart. "Go. Get to safety."

℘ 🚂 ℭ

"Is Daddy going to be okay?" Chloe asked. Her lower lip trembled and her beautiful blue Caldwell eyes pleaded for a positive answer.

Swallowing her tears, Erica forced herself to offer her daughter a smile. They had to get out fast. Jamie wouldn't be able to hold the beam up much longer. "Daddy's the best at his job, sweetie. Remember that." She nodded to Dani, who turned and began pulling the stretcher out of the void Chloe had been trapped in. Coco went ahead, sniffing out the easiest path.

Despite her injured foot, the cut in her thigh, and the tourniquet she'd had to improvise, they managed to get Chloe in the stretcher over the wall, using the ropes she and Dani had left behind on their way in. Fortunately, nothing blocked the hole Dani had drilled through the reinforced concrete either. Erica had a brief moment of despair when she saw that the two beams crossed in a V were now covered in a mountain of pipes, plaster, and wood. But Coco ran to the left and barked until they followed. The shifting caused by the aftershock had opened a different path, a much easier one with far fewer obstacles. Without pausing, they raced away from Jamie and the fallen I-beam.

Away from the man she loved.

After what felt like hours but was really only a few minutes, they exited where they'd entered and found two members of the team, Colin and Evan, waiting for them. The men each grabbed an end of the stretcher and ran the remaining distance to the stairs.

As soon as they entered the shelter of the stairwell, Dani instructed the men to tuck the stretcher along the wall and told Erica to hunker down. "We're clear, LJ," she said to Jamie over the radio.

Erica's heart clenched as she realized what was about to happen. Ignoring Dani, she stood and peered out the door to where Jamie continued to single-handedly hold up the I-beam that had almost killed them all. God. How could he do it? Illuminated by strong spotlights from the fourth floor, she saw his muscles bulging. Sweat soaked his hair and dripped down over his mask.

He looked up and his gaze held hers. After a moment, he stepped back and let the beam fall. The entire building shook, the noise deafening. Her heart pounding, her mind reeling, she watched in frozen disbelief as the floor caved and Jamie disappeared. Her knees gave out and she sank to the ground, screaming, "Jamie! Jamie, no!"

Her cries ripped through her throat, her entire body suddenly cold. This couldn't be happening. Jamie was a survivor. The best at his job. It couldn't end this way. Scrambling to her feet, she started running back the way she'd come. Maybe she could get to him. Maybe he was still alive.

Before she'd gone three yards, she was tackled from behind and fell face first on top of a broken desk.

"Erica, calm down," Dani said. "You can't go there."

"But, Jamie—"

Dani turned Erica's head and pointed. Out of the haze of dust and plaster, Jamie's limp body rose out of the hole in the floor suspended from a rope. Joy filled her chest to overflowing. He was alive. Jamie was going to be okay. Only...

"Dani! What's wrong with him?" He hung unmoving in the harness as his team pulled him up to the fourth floor.

When she turned to Dani, she saw the woman's pale face and sad eyes. "Hollywood? How is he?" she asked into the radio.

Not waiting for an answer, Erica spun on her heel and ran back into the stairwell and pointed to the lower levels. "Get Chloe out of the building. Now," she shouted to the men. Then she tore off in the opposite direction, bounding up the steps to the next floor as fast as she could with her bum leg. Colin tried to catch her, but she twisted and evaded his hold, bursting through the doors to the fourth floor.

No one was going to stop her. She needed to be with her husband.

Like a mad woman, she dashed through the dark rubble-ridden halls, her flashlight bobbing wildly. She hurdled mounds of broken office furniture, stumbled, tripped, and picked herself up again. Every obstacle fed her need to overcome, her need to be with Jamie.

After what felt like a marathon, she arrived panting and bleeding in the ruined common area, which now featured a gaping hole in the floor. Her legs weakened at the sight of the team hovering over Jamie's prone body. She staggered forward, pushing through the men, and fell to her knees beside Hollywood, who was carefully disengaging Jamie's harness. "Is he?" she asked in a whisper, unable to give voice to her worst fear.

Hollywood gave her a crooked smile as he removed Jamie's mask. "I think his lordship just needs a kiss from his lady to wake him up."

Dropping to the ground beside Jamie, she ripped off her own mask and took his hand. It was warm. His chest rose and fell in even beats. She leaned over, hugging him, tears flowing freely down her cheeks. "Thank God." She kissed his lips. Wonderful soft lips that had haunted her nights for the last year. "Did you hear that, Jamie? You're going to be fine. We're all going to be fine."

"Well, he's going to have a pretty sore head for a few days, and he probably has a concussion. But yeah, he'll live."

Frowning, she rose up and touched the swelling on the side of Jamie's head. His eyes popped open, and seeing her, he smiled. "Rickie."

"How are you feeling?" she asked gently.

"Glad to be alive."

"You got a nasty bump on your head. Why weren't you wearing your helmet?"

He reached his hand up and tapped her head with his knuckles, grinning.

Hearing the thud, she remembered. He'd given her his helmet. He'd wanted her to be safe. "I'm so sorry, Jamie."

"Shh... I did it because I wanted to. I'd give my life for yours."

"You almost did."

Hollywood coughed. "I hate to interrupt the reunion, but unless we get out of here ASAP, you still might."

Jamie struggled to sit up. Erica quickly tucked her shoulder under his and helped him to his feet.

After helping her put her mask back on, he smiled down at her. "Let's go see our daughter."

CHAPTER 8

Jamie sat on a stretcher at the foot of Medic 11, enduring his younger brother Chad's ministrations. He resisted and feigned annoyance like any older brother would do, but in reality, he was relieved to see Chad. Relieved to know his brother was safe. Chad had updated him on the rest of the family. William had been at his condo when the quake hit. That building, built to all the latest earthquake codes, had withstood the tremors without a single paint fleck. His parents and Victoria, Chad's twin, were also fine. Their older house in Queen Anne had sustained some damage, but they'd taken shelter in the reinforced bathroom he'd insisted they build.

Simmons and his security team gathered around Aid 44, where Colin and Evan cleaned wounds and bandaged injuries. Several people clearly in need of medical attention broke away from the crowd gathered in City Hall Park, next to the Courthouse, and approached the ambulances.

It was going to be a very long night.

Jamie looked over at the stretcher beside his where Rickie watched anxiously as Chad's partner, Liam, strapped Chloe's leg into a temporary brace while she kept a tight hold on her mother's hand. "How's she doing?" he asked.

Liam smiled at Chloe. "Leg's broken. But our little lass is taking it like her old man. She hasn't complained once," he said with a thick Irish brogue.

71

Chloe's face scrunched up and she giggled. "You sound funny, like a leprechaun."

Jamie slid off the stretcher and took her hand, winking. "Good thing he doesn't look like one though."

She studied Liam's face, then Chad's before nodding. "Good thing, 'cause Uncle Chad doesn't like leprechauns."

Everyone laughed. Except Hollywood. What was up with that? Whatever. Jamie had too much on his mind to worry about his friend's mood right now. He let go of Chloe's hand and moved back, giving Liam space to work, but still close enough to keep a watchful eye on his daughter. Rickie came to stand beside him and he laid a hand on her shoulder. "How are you doing?"

She leaned into him a little and looked up, her lips curving. "A lot better than I thought I would be an hour ago." Her smile fell and her bottom lip trembled. "I really thought we were all going to die."

He ran the back of his index finger along her cheek. "We wouldn't have all made it if you hadn't stepped in. You're one of the bravest women I've ever known."

She turned in his arms and laid her head on his chest. "About that trip…"

It took him a moment to figure out what she was talking about. The trip he'd suggested earlier. The trip she'd shot down. "What about it?"

"I think we should go."

"Sure. When Chloe's healed up, we can celebrate and take her to Disneyland. She'll love that."

Her chin lifted and she met his gaze. "I was thinking of something a little more adult."

Did she mean what he thought she meant? "Adult how?"

She ducked her head and tried to step out of his arms. He tightened his hold. No way was he letting her squirm out of this now. She'd started it, she was going to finish it. "I've got a concussion, Rickie. You're going to have to spell it out for me."

"I think we need some time alone. Like you said, some time to reconnect."

"So you want to go away for the weekend, something like that?"

"I was thinking something more along the lines of a proper honeymoon. We never did have one."

A honeymoon? Holy shit. Was she saying she wanted to get back together? His heart started hammering against his ribs and his breathing came in short huffs. *Take it easy, man. Don't scare her.* "What would we do with Chloe?" he asked, trying to sound casual.

She toyed with the fabric of his T-shirt. "I thought your mom might like to have her over for a visit."

Jamie stumbled and quickly covered it up by sitting on the bumper of the ambulance. "You sure you trust my mom to take care of Chloe while we're gone? It'll have to be at least a week."

Her gaze roamed from Jamie, to Drew and Chad. "I figure if she could cope with all you Caldwell boys, she can deal with Chloe."

Was he imagining all of this? If he was, he prayed never to wake up. But if this was real, then he had to clear up a few things. He'd made a lot of mistakes both in what he'd done and in what'd he'd accepted. He wasn't going to make the same mistakes again. He took her hand and pulled her down beside him. "If this is going to work, a few things need to change."

Her throat worked as she swallowed. "Like what?"

"Like I don't want to be an absentee father anymore. I want—no, I *need*—to be a part of Chloe's everyday life. A part of yours."

"I want that too."

"And you'll tell me if something I do bothers you?"

"Yes, and I'll expect you to do the same."

He put his arm around her shoulders and pulled her in for a kiss. As soon as her lips touched his, he knew he was in trouble. Love and lust surged through his veins, and he hardened almost to the point of pain. *Christ*, he wanted this woman. He wanted his *wife*. And after a long year of celibacy, he was finally going to have her. But not until they got home. Reluctantly, he softened the kiss and drew back. "Where do you want to go?"

"Go?"

Eyes glazed with arousal stared back at him. He grinned. "For our honeymoon."

"I don't much care." She smiled. "But no extreme adventure vacation please. I've had enough of that to last me a lifetime."

He tucked a loose strand of hair around her ear. "Come on. I'm sure you have some ideas." Rickie never proposed anything without having a clear idea of exactly what she wanted to do.

"Well, I've always wanted to visit London. I've already checked out all the tourist attractions."

He couldn't help the laugh that bubbled out of his chest. Rickie would change, but it would be a long road. "I bet you have an itinerary already planned."

A blush colored her cheeks. "Seven fun-filled days."

Unable to resist the show of vulnerability, he pressed his lips to hers once again. His hand slid into her hair and he held her neck, loving how she let him control the kiss. *Christ*, he'd missed her. Pulling back, he chuckled. "Seven fun-filled days in London sounds like an expedition to me. Remember how we talked about visiting Hawaii after Chloe was born?"

She ran her hand down his arm. "Sun, surf, drinks on the beach."

He slid his finger down her side, touching the curve of her breast. "Hot nights," he said, his voice husky.

"There are a few things I want to do if we go there."

His groin pulsed at the suggestion in her words. "Oh yeah? What?"

"Remember the first night we were together?"

He almost choked on his own tongue. That night had been magic for him. Something he'd never experienced before or since. He'd relived it thousands of times in his mind, always wishing he could relive it for real. But he'd always worried Rickie would run at the suggestion. "Are you saying that's something you'd like to try again?"

When she nodded, he swallowed. His voice was rough when he spoke. "You are a very cruel woman. How the hell am I going to survive until then?"

"Consider it an incentive." She threw him a saucy grin as she hopped to the ground, favoring her injured foot, and went to see their daughter.

Jamie returned the grin and slapped his hands together. Hot damn! He had his wife back. His woman. His hot *sexy* woman.

And seven days wasn't going to be nearly long enough to show her how much he'd missed her. With any luck—and his and Rickie's grit—they'd have a lifetime to enjoy each other. That might just be enough time to explore everything he wanted to do to her. Might just be enough.

Jamie and Erica's story continues in *Under His Command*, the first book in the Six-Alarm Sexy series. Read on for a special scorching hot preview!

A NOTE TO READERS

Thank you for reading *Aftershocks*. I hope you've enjoyed it!

If you enjoyed *Aftershocks*, please consider writing a review to help others learn about the book. Every recommendation helps, and I appreciate anyone who takes the time to share their love of books and reading with others. Feel free to follow me on Facebook, Twitter, or any of the other social media sites. I'm on almost all of them! I love to talk with readers about books, any books, not just my own. So, please, stop by for a chat.

I've started a reader group for fans of my books on Facebook. If you enjoy talking about books, reading sneak previews, and playing games, then this is the place you want to be!

www.facebook.com/groups/FansKristineCayneBooks

If once-in-a-while emails are more your style, you can sign up for my newsletter:

www.kristinecayne.com/Newsletter.html

Thank you for your support!

ABOUT THE AUTHOR

Kristine Cayne's books have won numerous awards and acclaim. Her first book, *Deadly Obsession*, was an *RT Book Reviews* Top Pick and won Best Romance in the 2012 eFestival of Words Best of the Independent eBook Awards. Her second book, *Deadly Addiction*, won two awards at the 2014 eFestival of Words and 1st place in the INDIE Awards, Romantic Suspense Category (a division of Chanticleer Book Reviews Blue Ribbon Writing Contests).

Her book *Under His Command* won Best BDSM Romance at the 2012 Sizzling Awards and was a finalist in the 2013 eFestival of Words and 2013 RONE (Reward of Novel Excellence) Awards, and her book *Everything Bared* was a finalist in the Erotic category of the I Heart Indie awards.

www.kristinecayne.com

Kristine Cayne Proudly Presents

UNDER HIS COMMAND

Book one of the Six-Alarm Sexy erotic romance series

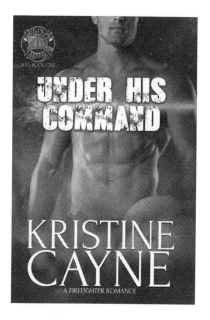

A firefighter desperate to save his failing marriage earns the trust—and the sexual submission—of his controlling wife in the most pleasurable of ways.

After an explosive one-night stand results in pregnancy, Jamie Caldwell is thrilled to marry the perfect foil to his Dom side. But when his submissive wife starts cringing every time he gives a command, Jamie shackles his dark desires. A bout of rough, frenzied reunion sex makes him wonder if now he should free the Dom he's kept in chains and teach Erica the joys of submission and sexual surrender.

Erica Caldwell secretly loved every sinful thing Jamie did to her on their first night together. However, terrified she'll become a codependent doormat like her mother, she repeatedly rejects Jamie's dominance, despite craving the kind of release only he can give her—the release that comes from yielding to Jamie's every demand.

Hoping that the trust required by BDSM will help them rebuild their faith in each other, Jamie and Erica embark on a journey of sexual exploration. But is it too late to repair their crumbling marriage?

Praise for Kristine Cayne's *Under His Command*

"Ms Cayne depicts beautifully this blossoming dom/sub relationship encompassing in its entirety a love hidden under guilt, courtesy and self-imposed expectations, Her ability to intoxicate the reader with her extensive array of sensually charged scene provokes an out of body experience.

I can't wait to see what comes next in this breathtaking series I was definitely left wanting much, much more!!"
—Nevena Read, Amazon review

"This book: It was... perfect... Just perfect. There are no words! I am speechless. Grateful. Amazed. WOW. Just...wow!

I LOVE this story. It's got just the right amount of edge, a strong female lead character, and a male lead who loves, cherishes, and RESPECTS his wife. It's what 50 Shades of Grey SHOULD have been but wasn't." —Amazon reader review

EXCERPT – UNDER HIS COMMAND

Chapter 1

Seattle, five years ago

Jamie Caldwell shoved open the door to his apartment, tugging the woman along behind him. As soon as she cleared the door, he kicked it shut, then lifted her up and pressed her back against it. When she licked her lips, drawing his attention to their fleshy plumpness, lust turned his blood to lava. He couldn't wait another minute to taste her, to have her. "You're so fucking sexy," he growled against her throat.

The girl—she'd said her name was Rickie—tilted her head to the side and moaned. The sound vibrated through him, electrifying him. Sliding his leg between hers, he lowered her until she was riding his thigh, her heat scorching him even through his jeans. He pulled her blouse up over her face and paused for a moment, caught by the temptation to leave it across her eyes, before he yanked it off.

Her hips stopped their rocking motion and something flashed in her gaze. Uncertainty? He took her face in his hands and gently touched his lips to hers. No sense in scaring her off.

She wrapped her arms around his neck and pressed herself tightly against him. Taking that as a sign she wanted more, he twisted a hand in her blonde hair and used his grip to pull her head back before pushing his tongue into her mouth. She tasted sweet, like fruit. He'd bet anything she'd been drinking one of those girly vodka coolers at the party. On her, he liked it. Loved it, even.

When his tongue swept over hers, the groan that escaped her lips sent a jolt of arousal from his mouth to his cock. If he didn't get out of these jeans soon, he'd be stuck waiting for his hard-on to go away. And as long as she was around, that wasn't happening.

Setting her on the floor, he took her hand and drew her down the hall to his bedroom. He didn't have much in the way of furniture, but the sturdy four-poster custom-made king bed from Caldwell Fine Furnishings had been the first item he'd bought when he'd moved in. She eyed the bed curiously, then ran her hand over the smooth wooden footboard. "Wow, I didn't expect this."

What didn't she expect? Good furniture in a firefighter's house? Anger started to get the better of him, but then he remembered that she didn't even know what he did for a living. Before bringing her home, he'd made sure she wasn't a fire bunny. He'd had enough of those to last a lifetime. Taking a deep breath, he pushed the chip off his shoulder. "What do you mean?" he asked.

"I didn't expect to be making love on a Caldwell original." She grinned and turned to him. "My own bed is from IKEA. This is going to be a treat."

He wanted to smile, to respond to her teasing, but first, he needed to be sure she didn't know who he was. "How do you know it's a Caldwell?"

"My roommate. She couldn't stand the dorm beds, so she replaced it with hers from home. She literally spent hours telling me why Caldwells were the best and showing me how to identify them."

"So you're still in school. How old are you?" Shit. If she wasn't at least twenty-one, she was going home.

Her chin jutted out. "I'm old enough."

"How. Old."

"Almost twenty-two, okay?"

Phew. "What are you studying?" he asked, keeping his tone conversational. If the lady wanted some chitchat before they got serious, so be it.

"Pre-law, here at UW."

His brows flew up. "You want to be a lawyer?"

Her smile fell and she turned away. "Only if I can get in with a scholarship. The money I make working at the cafeteria certainly won't pay for law school." She chuckled then, but it sounded strained.

Jamie knew all about financial woes. The Caldwell clan had grown up happy, but they'd never had any excess cash. When Grandpa Bill died, Jamie's father had taken over as CEO of Caldwell Fine Furnishings. Unfortunately, he'd always been more interested in the latest chair design than in the bottom-line, so the company had struggled. Although Jamie's parents had encouraged him to get a degree, he'd dropped out and joined the SFD to pitch in with his younger brother William's tuition. Helping William become a CPA had been the right decision for the whole family and for the business. William was slowly whipping the company into shape, and when their dad eventually stepped down as CEO, everyone expected William to take his place.

Jamie slipped his hands around the girl's waist, enjoying the feel of her smooth flat stomach, and ran his tongue along the side of her neck. Her breath hitched and her nipples pebbled through the baby blue lace of her bra. "Maybe you just need to find yourself a rich husband who can make all your dreams come true," he murmured, using his breath to tickle her skin. Her shiver was his reward.

"Someone like you?" she asked and pushed her ass against him.

He snorted. "Hardly." After six years in the fire service, he made decent money, but no one would ever think of him as rich.

She squeezed her hand between their bodies and stroked his erection. "Speaking of hard..."

That was all the urging he needed. He spun her around and brought his mouth down on hers in a demanding kiss. The taste of her did crazy things to his body. His heart raced as though he'd just run up the practice tower in full gear, and he could barely think with wanting to be inside her.

He lifted his head and backed her up until her legs hit the bed frame. Before they started, he had to make something very clear, just in case there was some truth to their joking. "Tonight is for fun. No strings, no expectations, no limits. Agreed?"

Her eyes clouded for a moment before she nodded. "Agreed."

The word was barely out of her mouth when he gave her a little push to make her fall back on the bed. She was still gasping when he grabbed the waistband of her jeans and yanked them off her legs. The matching blue panties drew his attention. Placing his hands on her thighs, he drew them apart. She made a slight show of resistance, but gave that up when he frowned at her. Through the delicate material, he could see the shadowed outline of her folds, but no dark hair showed through. Was she truly blonde? Or shaved? Either would work. He grinned. "Take off your bra."

When she sat up, her legs drifted together. He tapped her right knee. "Keep your legs open."

Her eyes widened, but she did as he asked. The movement transfixed him like the unwrapping of a long-awaited gift. His gaze wandered up to her chest and focused there while she undid the bra clasp at her back. What tumbled out took his breath away. Perfectly pale, perfectly rose-tipped.

"Do you know how pretty you are?" he murmured.

She shook her head and started to close her legs again, but when she looked up at him, she stopped herself. Good, she was catching on.

"Lie back," he said. After she complied, he slid two fingers into the sides of her panties and tugged them down to expose her. The very narrow, very fine strip of pale hair left the outer pink lips clearly visible. How would she taste? He was more than eager to find out.

When he finished removing her panties, she immediately spread her legs wide. He smiled and rewarded her by kneeling between her thighs and tracing his finger along her silken folds. "You have a gorgeous pussy."

Her snort caught him by surprise. "You don't think so?" he asked.

"First, it's not gorgeous, and second, I hate that word."

"Pussy? What else should I call it? Crotch? Mound?" His mock-shudder made her laugh. The low throaty sound had him imagining what noises she'd make when she came. Christ. His cocked pulsed against his zipper.

"I guess there is no good word for it. But men use pussy in such a vulgar way. It's always turned me off."

With the tip of his finger, he massaged the V along both sides of her clit. The tender skin gleamed with her juices, and she writhed beneath his touch. "You don't seem turned off to me." A blush bloomed on her cheeks. She really was too cute. He continued his exploration. "Let's see. It's soft and warm and furry, and it likes to be petted. When you do it just right, you even hear it purr." He ran his finger up to her clit and circled around it.

"Mmm," she closed her eyes and moaned.

"Sounds like a pussy to me."

Her lids popped open and her gaze shot to his face. She answered his grin with one of her own. "You do have a way with... words, Jamie." She licked her lips and arched her back.

"But we'd better get this show on the road. I'm pretty close to the edge already."

Was she now? Little Rickie was going to learn that, with him, orgasms had to be earned, and she hadn't earned hers yet. Far from it. He stepped back from the bed and undid his jeans, letting his cock pop free. She sat up and watched as he wrapped his hand around it and stroked its length. "Want this?" he asked.

She swallowed and cleared her throat before answering. "Y-yes."

"Then come and get it."

Rising from the bed, she crossed the few feet over to him and stopped. When she reached out to touch him, he shook his head. "On your knees." The words tore out of his throat, thick and hoarse with need.

He waited for her to follow through on his command before removing his jeans and boxers. He tossed them onto the chair by the window then went back to her, placing the head of his cock so that it barely touched her glistening lips. A drop of pre-cum escaped. Her tongue peeked out from her alluring mouth and she licked up the bead with one broad swipe, a satisfied smile on her face. His knees shook with the strength of his arousal.

Who was this woman?

To hide his surprise, he wrapped a hank of her hair around his hand and tugged until her head fell back, then he moved in close. "Suck me. Deep."

ᔕ 🚗 ᔐ

This night was going to kill her.

Erica Madden gripped the sheets on Jamie's Caldwell original bed and turned her face into the pillow, clenching her teeth to muffle her screams—screams of ecstasy. She'd come so many times, she'd lost count. All she could do was lie there limp and satisfied.

But Jamie had other ideas.

He flipped her onto her stomach, then wrapped an arm around her waist and pulled her hips up so her ass was pressed against his cock. His still very hard cock. "On all fours, baby," he ground out, the raw hunger in his voice like the rasp of a tongue along her spine. She shivered and wondered how he could possibly expect her to keep going.

Something soft and cool slid over her eyes. "What's this?" she asked, reaching for it.

"Shh… It's just a blindfold. To heighten your senses."

Like she needed her senses heightened? He'd already taken her places she'd never been. "I'm not sure about—"

His hand smacking her butt cheek completely derailed her train of thought. "Did you just slap me?"

"That was a spank. Now turn around." He tied the scarf over her eyes, plunging her into darkness.

She really should resist, tell him to stop. Something. But she didn't. "Okay. Why should I let you spank me?" she asked. So far this night had been like nothing she'd expected. Jamie was skilled and unpredictable. And she was genuinely curious.

"Because you love it." His fingers trailed down the crease between her cheeks and dipped into her. Her body convulsed, pushing against his hand to take more of him. What was it about fingers that felt so darned good?

Another smack, this one a little harder, had her trembling. "See how wet you are? How good it feels?" he said.

He was so right. His hand, brushing her butt, was cool in comparison to her heated skin. And his fingers deep inside her found that most sensitive of spots, massaging it in tight circles.

With the scarf covering her eyes, she lost all perception of time, of place, of self, of everything except the enthralling sensation of his fingers stroking inside her and the low rumble of his voice. She could go on like this forever.

She moaned in protest when he pulled his fingers out of her, but she sighed in pleasure when he replaced them with his cock. He wrapped one hand around her hair and tugged until she arched her back, then he pulled her in tight against him with his other hand, his fingers grasping her hip.

In this position, he seemed even longer—impossibly long— as he glided in and out of her, the occasional swivel of his hips driving her crazy. Her breath hitched when he released her hair and his hands cupped her breasts. His strong fingers teased her nipples with light flicks of his nails before he caught the tips between his knuckles and squeezed. Gently at first. But as the speed of his thrusts increased, so did the pressure on her nipples.

"I can't take anymore!" she cried.

"You can and you will. You'll take everything I give you."

Yes! She clamped her lips together to keep from shouting out her answer as he tweaked and pulled on the tight peaks, making her walk that fine line between pleasure and pain. Yes, he was right. She would take it all, and if she didn't stop herself, she might even beg him for it.

Deprived as she was of sight, her sense of touch increased. Every slip, every slide, every heated caress became her only connection with the world, with reality. What was this man doing to her? She'd always enjoyed sex, but she'd never experienced anything like this before. It was a mind-blowing, full-body experience. Maybe even a life-changing one.

Tension coiled inside her. Eager now, almost desperate to reach the edge and jump over it, she rocked her hips against him, urging him to go deeper, faster. He spanked her again. Blood rushed to the spot, and her juices flowed. She groaned, the pleasure almost unbearable. What was wrong with her that she wanted him to do it again?

He pushed her face into the pillow and pressed a burning hand on her back to keep her in place. "Stay."

His gruffly spoken command echoed with his desire, his arousal. Jamie was clearly on the edge right beside her. As his cock slammed into her again and again, the pressure built higher and higher. Was this what heaven felt like?

Just as she thought she'd die from the intense sensations, she felt him swell inside her—could he really get any bigger? She contracted her pelvic muscles and screamed into the pillow as a powerful climax sent her soaring. Jamie continued to grip her hips and pound into her, extending her orgasm, catapulting her into another one.

He plunged into her several more times, shuddering with his own release. Her knees gave out under his weight and she dropped onto the mattress. He followed her down, but before she could be crushed under his weight, it was gone. Where was he?

"Come here," he whispered, rolling her over and pulling her into his arms.

₭ 🚃 ℒ

Erica woke feeling trapped. Something heavy pressed across her stomach and her legs. And even though her eyes were open, she couldn't see a thing. Her heart thundered in her chest as she tried to get her bearings and recall where she was, what had happened the previous night.

Jamie.

When she remembered what they'd done, her face burned and her *pussy* quivered. Maybe he was right about that word. The way he'd said it, the tone of his voice—the reverence—had made it sound almost... cute.

One of her hands seemed to be stuck, but the other was free. She brought it to her eyes and felt the silky material. Jamie had blindfolded her that last time they'd made love. Correction: they'd fucked. And she'd loved every minute.

Realizing she must still be at Jamie's apartment, she yanked off the blindfold. And there he lay: his dark hair too short to be ruffled, his closed lids hiding baby blues, and his jaw relaxed in sleep. He was tall, tanned, beautifully muscled, and sprawled over her, as though he wanted to keep her near. She shook off the stupid romantic notion. He'd made it clear last night—no strings, no expectations, no limits. They'd certainly managed that last requirement. Now it was time for her to fulfill the first two by leaving before he woke up. Mornings after were uncomfortable. Not that she'd had many, but this was one she preferred to avoid.

Maybe she could find out where he worked or where he hung out and arrange a chance encounter. If they met again under more normal circumstances, she'd see if he was still interested in her. Last night had been fantasy-shattering. She could only wonder what it would be like to get to know him, to take things slow and see where the relationship went.

Carefully, she eased his arm off her stomach and slid sideways, freeing her legs. When he made a noise, she froze and waited to see if he'd awaken. Luckily, he rolled onto his side, away from her, liberating her trapped arm in the process.

She paused for a moment to admire his sculpted back and what it had felt like to run her hands along all that restrained strength. This was the first time she'd slept with someone more than a year or two older than she was. Not that he was ancient or anything, but after him, every guy at school would seem like a boy. Jamie was a man in his prime and he'd proven that to her over and over again. Her entire body tingled just from the sight of him.

Spinning around, she grabbed her discarded clothes and tiptoed out of the bedroom to the sunny living room. Her shirt lay on the floor near the door. As she fastened her bra and pulled her blouse on, some pictures on the wall caught her attention. This might be her only chance to discover the identity of this man, this sexual paragon.

A photograph of Jamie in a spiffy navy blue uniform drew her like a magnet. Was he a cop? She peered at it closely and read the inscription on the badge. SFD. Jamie was a firefighter. In a rush, their conversation from the previous night came back to her. No wonder he'd been so insistent about knowing her age. He probably thought she was one of those women who threw herself at firefighters, hoping to land a husband. The men made good money and had great benefits. How could he not think she was one of them after what she'd said in response to his teasing about finding a rich husband to pay for her school? *Someone like you*, she'd said.

She needed to leave. Right away.

But as she stepped into her panties, she noticed a photo of Jamie with his arm around a young woman who gazed up at him, love shining in her eyes. The photo appeared recent. All residual arousal left her body in a cold rush. Did Jamie have a girlfriend? A wife? She twisted, taking in the rest of the room, searching for signs of a feminine touch. Her heart dropped when she spotted the plant on the coffee table, the colored cushions on the sofa.

Damn. Damn. How could she have been so stupid? Too busy drowning in her attraction to him, she hadn't even *asked* if he was involved with someone. *No strings, no expectations.* His words made perfect sense now. Fuming, she squirmed into her jeans. He'd used her. Good thing she'd told him her name was

Rickie, and he didn't know her last name. He'd never be able to track her down, even if he bothered to try.

No matter how great he was in bed, she knew she'd never be—could never be—more than a one-night stand for someone like him. She deserved more. She deserved better.

www.kristinecayne.com

Continue reading for a special preview of Kristine Cayne's first Deadly Vices novel

DEADLY OBSESSION

When an Oscar-winning movie star meets a department-store photographer...

Movie star Nic Lamoureux appears to have a playboy's perfect life. But it's a part he plays, an act designed to conceal a dark secret he carries on his shoulders. His empty days and nights are a meaningless blur until he meets the woman who fulfills all his dreams. She and her son are the family he's always wanted—if she can forgive a horrible mistake from his past.

A Hollywood dream...

Lauren James, a widowed single mother, earns barely enough money to support herself and her son. When she wins a photography contest and meets Nic, the man who stars in all her fantasies, her dreams, both professional and personal, are on the verge of becoming real. The attraction between Lauren and Nic is instant—and mutual. Their chemistry burns out of control during a photo shoot that could put Lauren on the fast track to a lucrative career.

Becomes a Hollywood nightmare

But an ill-advised kiss makes front-page news, and the lurid headlines threaten everything Nic and Lauren have hoped for. Before they know what's happening, their relationship is further rocked by an obsessed and cunning stalker who'll stop at nothing—not even murder—to have Nic to herself. When Nic falls for Lauren, the stalker zeroes in on her as the competition. And the competition must be eliminated.

An excerpt from *Deadly Obsession*

Lauren rolled her eyes. "Fine. Do it."

Nic bent down and brushed his lips against hers. For the first few seconds, she didn't kiss him back, but she didn't push him away, either. Then, on a sigh, she leaned into him and her arms locked around his neck. His tongue darted out to taste her bottom lip. Mmm... cherry—his new favorite flavor. When her mouth opened, he didn't hesitate.

He dove in. And drowned.

He'd meant this to be a quick kiss, only now he just couldn't stop. His lips traced a path to her throat. Cupping her bottom with his hands, he lifted her up, grinding against her. She moaned. It was a beautiful sound, one he definitely wanted to hear again.

A loud noise pierced the fog of his lust. He raised his head from where he'd been nuzzling Lauren's apple-scented neck to tell whoever it was to fuck off, but as the sexual haze cleared, he swallowed the words. The paparazzi had gathered around, applauding and calling out crude encouragements. Some snapped photos while others rolled film. Shit. He'd pay for this fuck-up and so would she.

www.kristinecayne.com

92

Continue reading for a special preview of Dana Delamar's first Blood and Honor novel

REVENGE

A woman on the run...

Kate Andretti is married to the Mob—but doesn't know it. When her husband uproots them to Italy, Kate leaves everything she knows behind. Alone in a foreign land, she finds herself locked in a battle for her life against a husband and a family that will "silence" her if she will not do as they wish. When her husband tries to kill her, she accepts the protection offered by a wealthy businessman with Mafia ties. He's not a mobster, he claims. Or is he?

A damaged Mafia don...

Enrico Lucchesi never wanted to be a Mafia don, and now he's caught in the middle of a blood feud with the Andretti family. His decision to help Kate brings the feud between the families to a boil. When Enrico is betrayed by someone in his own family, the two of them must sort out enemies from friends—and rely on each other or die alone. The only problem? Enrico cannot reveal his identity to Kate, or she'll bolt from his protection, and he'll be duty-bound to kill her to safeguard his family's secret.

A rival bent on revenge...

Attacks from without and within push them both to the breaking point, and soon Enrico is forced to choose between protecting the only world he knows and saving the woman he loves.

Praise for Dana Delamar

"Here is to a WHOOPING 5 Stars. If I had to describe this book in about four words, it would be action-packed, sexy, romantic, and adrenaline rushing...." —*Bengal Reads* blog, 5 stars

An Excerpt from *Revenge*

Enrico raised a hand in greeting to Kate, and she returned his wave and started descending the steps.

She headed straight for him, her auburn hair gleaming in the sun, a few strands of it blowing across her pale cheek and into her green eyes. With a delicate hand, she brushed the hair out of her face. Enrico's fingers twitched with the desire to touch her cheek like that, to feel the slide of her silky hair. A small, almost secretive, smile crossed her features, and he swallowed hard. *Dio mio.* He felt that smile down to his toes.

She stopped a couple feet from him. "Signor Lucchesi, it's good to see you, as always."

He bowed his head slightly. "And you, Signora Andretti." He paused, a grin spreading across his face. "Since when did we get so formal, Kate?"

She half-turned and motioned to the doorway behind her. And that was when he noticed it—a bruise on her right cheek. *Merda! Had someone hit her?* Tearing his eyes off the mark, he followed her gesture. A tall, sandy-haired man, well-muscled and handsome, leaned in the doorway, his arms crossed. "My husband, Vincenzo, is here."

Enrico's smile receded. He looked back to Kate. "I'd like to meet him." *And if he did this to you, he's going to pay.*

www.danadelamar.com

Made in the USA
Columbia, SC
29 September 2019